Just [illegible] trouble I Needed

THE BAYOU SABINE SERIES

JUST THE TROUBLE I NEEDED

The Bayou Sabine Series

LAUREN FAULKENBERRY

Publisher's Cataloging-in-Publication Data
Faulkenberry, Lauren 1978-.
Just the Trouble I Needed : A Bayou Sabine Novella / Lauren Faulkenberry.
p.____ cm.____
ISBN 978-1-947834-02-6 (Pbk) | ISBN 978-1-947834-03-3 (eBook)
1. Women—Louisiana—Fiction. 2. Love—Fiction. 3. Dogs—Fiction. I. Title.
813'.6—dc23 | 2017952975

Blue Crow Books

Published by Blue Crow Books
an imprint of Blue Crow Publishing, LLC
Chapel Hill, NC
www.bluecrowpublishing.com
Cover Design by Lauren Faulkenberry

Praise for The Bayou Sabine Series

Beautifully descriptive and engaging. A delightful story about learning to let go of who you think you need to be and take a risk on happiness.

—Orly Konig, author of THE DISTANCE HOME and founding president of the Women's Fiction Writers Association.

Faulkenberry is a gifted storyteller with the ability to capture the most human side of relationships. *Bayou Whispers* is a rich and emotional story that will draw readers into the heat of the bayou and leave them wanting more.

-Tina Ann Forkner, award-winning author of THE REAL THING and WAKING UP JOY

I'd read this book again, and I recommend it to others who love a fast-paced romantic mystery. I give this book five stars.

- Dayna Leigh Cheser, author of the TIME series

I loved this book. It has so many different dimensions that you will literally be glued to the pages...There's mystery, intrigue, and unexpected pieces to the story. PICK UP THIS BOOK. It's a MUST READ.

- Pretty Little Book Reviews

From the moment Jack spoke in that French/Creole drawl he and Faulkenberry had me hook, line and sinker. I was a goner, and I didn't surface until the novel's end. I may be in love.

- Page One Books

Faulkenberry creates a world of magic, suspense, and desire. An engrossing romance with just the right amount of heat!

- Julie C. Gardner, author of LETTERS FOR SCARLET

Also by Lauren Faulkenberry

The Bayou Sabine Series:

BAYOU MY LOVE

BACK TO BAYOU SABINE

BAYOU WHISPERS

JUST THE TROUBLE I NEEDED

Other Fiction:

BENEATH OUR SKIN and Other Stories

sign up for Lauren's author newsletter,

Writing Down South:

tinyletter.com/firebrandpress

for Andrew

Chapter One

THE KITCHEN LOOKED like the scene of a crime. It wasn't even my kitchen, but it made me sick just the same. A red puddle covered the floor at the point of impact, a sunburst of my famous marinara sauce. The casserole dish had broken into three big pieces, but I knew I'd be picking up ceramic splinters for the next week. Slices of eggplant and floppy lasagna noodles were strewn in front of the stove, but not nearly enough to have filled the dish.

My bottle of shiraz lay on its side, teetering on the edge of the counter by the stove. Thankfully, I had put the cork back in it before I went upstairs to take a bath. The bath had been my treat for surviving my first full day here in the land of giant mosquitoes and prehistoric reptiles. This week was supposed to be relaxing, but it was off to a terrible start.

For a moment I thought the disaster was my fault. In my rush to relax in the bath, had I left the stove eye on, absentmindedly placed the dish on top of it and caused it to explode? I'd been unfocused lately, most days feeling like I was in someone else's skin, someone else's life. Since stalking out of the research facility last Friday, I'd envisioned a lot of things exploding: the toilets in the employee lounge, the line of test tubes in my lab, even my colleague Ray, who constantly leered at me over the rims of his wayfarer glasses.

I'd sometimes fantasized about having a lab accident that would give me a supernatural ability that was both useful and a little dangerous. Some days I wished I was like that girl in the Stephen King book who could start fires just by squinting her eyes and concentrating. If I had that power though, I wouldn't waste it on baked pasta. No, I would use it on the pants of people like Ray. And my boss Jeffrey, who so easily told me my job was about to be eliminated, and my ex, Benjamin, who'd dumped me right before Christmas and still continued to call and text me, whining about his bad decision and its unhappy repercussions, all of which I could have predicted.

Too bad I hadn't been able to predict how he would mistreat me.

I thought I'd gotten over him, but when Jeffrey called me into his office last Friday and told me the lab's funding was being cut, the familiar teeth of betrayal began gnawing at me once again. The blood had risen in my cheeks as Jeffrey explained that they were cutting several positions, making them intermittent contract work instead. They might be able to bring me back in a consulting role, but it would be only part-time. No benefits. I'd spent the last hour of my workday staring into a centrifuge, watching samples spin and separate, and my rage had bloomed into a kind of recognition: I hated my job. There was a time when I'd liked it, but it wasn't a challenge anymore. I'd lost sight of what I wanted, stuck in the spin of the lab. But it had given me stability and predictability: two things I needed most.

I surveyed the kitchen, examining the scene. The stove's dials were off. A noodle squished under my toes. Then a single red paw print caught my eye.

"Bella!" I yelled, stomping into the living room.

It felt weird walking around and yelling in a house that wasn't mine, but Enza had told me to make myself at home. Enza, my best friend, had called me on Friday night. I hadn't planned to tell her about my job, because Enza's a fixer. She's a sweetheart, for sure, but her first inclination is always to offer support, quickly followed by plans to rebuild. She flips houses for a living, so she's used to fixing broken things and making them like new again.

I just wasn't in the mood to have her trying to fix me.

For the first time since college, I was uncertain about my future. Uncertain about what I wanted from it. When Enza called, I avoided the topic of work as long as possible.

"Are you seeing anybody new?" she asked. I could imagine her twirling that dark curly hair of hers around her fingers as she spoke.

"Not really," I said.

"Kate," she groaned. "You have to get out of that lab more often. You're too much fun to be a workaholic."

I tugged at the ends of my hair, thinking it was time for a cut. After a whole winter inside, it was a dark shade of blond—the shade that indicates no sunlight for a year. I didn't even get any tan lines last summer.

"I know," I said.

"Sometimes I picture you as a mad scientist, like a Jekyll and Hyde situation."

"I'm definitely feeling more like Hyde today."

"Seriously," she said. "You never take a vacation. They must owe you three months by now."

It was more like four. Which was how I ended up getting this week away. Jeffrey had hesitated at first, but if he hadn't conceded to my request, I'd been prepared to pack my lab up into a couple of banker's boxes and hustle out like the building was on fire, leaving my current project incomplete. Jeffrey didn't appreciate unfinished experiments. That had been my one bargaining chip.

"Don't worry," I said. "I think things are about to change."

"Sure," Enza said. I could tell from her tone how high her eyebrow was arched.

"No, really. I'm on vacation starting today."

Enza shrieked, and I held the phone away from my ear. "Tell me more," she said. "Where are you going? What's the plan?"

"No solid plans," I said.

Enza was chattering so fast I could hardly keep up. "I'm so happy," she said. "No one deserves a nice vacation more than you. After all the overtime, all the holidays, all the breakthroughs—you're the smartest person they've got and it's about time they did something nice for you."

I finished my glass of wine in one long swallow. "Nice doesn't accurately describe it," I said, and then I couldn't lie to her anymore. I told her about how Jeffrey had told me the grant money was being reallocated this year and then used that ridiculous word. *We're downsizing,* he'd said, as if they were moving the three-story lab to a smaller building, or clearing out all the old equipment that was no longer useful. As he talked about coming back in a part-time capacity, his pig-like eyes had darted past me as if he couldn't wait to get me out of the room.

Enza was quiet for a long moment. I poured another glass of wine, feeling just barely tipsy from the first.

"Hello?" I said. "Are you still there?"

"I have an idea," she said. "Jack and I are leaving town on Monday for a little getaway ourselves. Why don't you come here and house-sit? Forget about all of that work nonsense for a while and swim in the lake."

"Your lake is full of dinosaurs with big, pointy teeth. I saw how that movie ended."

"Come on, Kate. Get out of the city for a while. You need some peace and quiet. And some nature, for god's sake." What she was really saying: *You never leave Raleigh. You never take time for yourself. And put your big girl panties on.*

She wasn't wrong.

"It's hotter than hell down there," I said. And it was. Enza lived in Bayou Sabine, a little town close to New Orleans. She'd insisted I visit her last Christmas after my breakup with Benjamin. I would have just walked around in my underwear if her boyfriend and her entire family hadn't been there. She had a big Victorian house that she'd inherited from her grandmother, more square footage than I could ever afford in Raleigh. It was like a dollhouse: big rooms with high ceilings and carved molding, a dozen acres, and a little lagoon that looked like something out of a movie shot with a fuzzy lens.

"It's cool in April," Enza said. "This is the best time to come. You'd be doing me a favor. You can watch the dog for us."

"I don't know."

"I bet there's a sheriff who'd be happy to see you," she said. "See? Everybody wins."

I groaned, thinking of the perfect storm last December that had shoved me into the orbit of the town sheriff, Andre. He was about as far from my type as I could get, but not as easy to resist as I'd predicted. He was kind and warm, two things I'd learned that Benjamin was not. Andre made me laugh, and he beat me at Scrabble, two things that made him exceptionally rare. But he lived in a tiny town in Louisiana that had zero use for someone like me, a person who peered into microscopes and petri dishes all day. This was the worst thing about dating at my age: I was stable, comfortable in my career and content with my status as a homeowner, and a cozy distance from my family. The problem with being thirty-four was that most men I encountered were also in that position, which made it difficult for either party to give up their work or home life for the sake of romantic risk. It was easy enough dating someone in my hometown, but to find a man in a different location that would upset the balance of everything? That seemed impossible.

Andre had been a welcome distraction from my breakup. We'd left things on friendly terms, never giving a definition to whatever we had. It was fun, and I liked him. But I didn't see how either of us could leave our careers to be together. After enough weeks had passed, I'd convinced myself that our parting was for the best. After Benjamin, it was clear that my judgment had been compromised. The last thing I needed now was another man complicating my life.

Besides, Andre was Jack's best friend. That made things much more complex. If Andre ended up hurt, then Jack would hate me, and that would put Enza in a difficult position.

No, it was best to stay away from the sheriff.

"I don't need a matchmaker, Enza."

"Have you heard from him?"

"Stop," I said. "No sheriff."

"Fine. Sit by the lake. Work on your tan. Read that stack of dirty novels you've been saving."

I took another sip of wine, trying not to think of Andre. But there he was with his hopelessly tousled hair, his wiry forearms, and his eyes that darkened when he laughed.

Dammit.

"I'm looking up flights right now," Enza said. "Direct from Raleigh-Durham, less than three hundred bucks. How's eight next Monday morning?"

"Ugh. That's too early."

"Otherwise you have to wait until four, and when you wait that long, the airline has time to run late, have catastrophes, and get delayed. Just get yourself some strong coffee and a doughnut. Maybe a cab so you don't get road rage."

I started to protest again, but thoughts of the blue-green lagoon seeped into my head, and I felt the lush grass beneath my toes, the tingle of sunlight on my skin, and then I was reading Enza the numbers on my credit card.

And now here I was, staring down a speckled swamp dog in my best friend's living room. Her coat was mottled gray and brown, like granite. Her amber eyes held a mix of curiosity and ire. "She likes you," Enza had cooed only yesterday, letting the beast lick her face. "She's super smart, and a great watchdog. You'll get along just fine."

But I could tell that dog hated me. She didn't lick my face. She didn't nuzzle me on the couch. She squinted at me the way my great aunt did when my three rambunctious brothers and I came to visit, bringing more baggage than Amtrak with us. Enza said it took a while for the dog to form a bond, that she was protective of her and Jack, and therefore wary of interlopers.

"She'll come around," Enza had said. "And I think you could use a loyal companion, since you insist on avoiding the sheriff." Bella was a catahoula, a herding breed that needed ample time outside to romp around and unearth trouble. When Jack and Enza had loaded up the car to leave, Bella had tried to herd them right back inside the house. She was clearly displeased when I was the one who went back inside with her.

"There you are," I said to the dog, my hands on my hips. "I saw what you did. Don't try to pretend it wasn't you."

Bella stood by the fireplace, peeking into my new leopard print tote bag that I'd bought the day I'd left the lab in an attempt to cheer myself up. She pricked her ears toward me, then looked away as if ashamed.

"Hey!" I said. "Get away from there."

Bella pushed her snout into the bag, still peering at me through one handle. She blinked at me once, woefully, and turned back to the bag, her ears flattened.

Her back arched as she emptied the contents of her stomach into the tote.

"Good god damn," I said.

The dog blinked at me and then stared at the wall.

"That was vintage, you little minx."

Bella snorted and shoved her nose into the bag. Her bobbed tail wagged.

I knew in that moment, as surely as I knew anything in my life, that I was not a dog person.

Chapter Two

I'D SWORN I wouldn't disturb Enza on her getaway, but this was an emergency. Bella had sprawled on her side by the fireplace, emitting monstrous sounds. I could only imagine the chemical reactions that were happening in that furry little body. Less than twenty-four hours in her house, and I'd broken the dog.

I sent her a text message: *Your dog hates me.*

After a few moments, she wrote: *Jack's dog.*

She barfed in my new tote bag.

Why?

Seriously? Dog people. *Because she hates me,* I wrote.

She's not a cat. She doesn't vomit for vengeance.

I groaned.

Did she get outside and eat some dead thing? Enza wrote.

She ate my eggplant lasagna. Do you think she needs a vet?

Your lasagna's not that bad.

You're hilarious.

Gotta run. Don't worry. She's had worse. She'll eat anything that sits still long enough.

I think we've made a terrible mistake, I wrote.

She'll like you more tomorrow. xoxo. Call Lucille if you need backup.

Lucille was Jack's younger cousin, who might as well have been his little sister. Jack's aunt and uncle had raised him right along with her after his parents had died. Enza had planned on inviting Lucille to house-sit before Friday's phone call changed that. Lucille had left me her phone number and said to call if I wanted company.

This getaway had become a disaster. I did need backup.

I texted Lucille: *Does anyone deliver pizza out here?*

She replied a few moments later. *LOL. Not where you are.*

Up for a girls' night out? Dog ruined my dinner and I'm starving.

Sure! I'll come pick you up. You're on the way to town.

What's in town?

Best seafood ever. Be there in twenty minutes.

Bella stared at me from across the room. She lay on her side, her legs splayed out as if she'd just tipped over like one of those fainting goats that go stiff as a board and crash to the earth out of fright. Her golden eyes were fixed on me as she let out a heavy sigh.

"Don't look at me like that," I said. "You brought this on yourself, you big piglet."

I went upstairs to change out of my pajamas. It was still warm out, so I chose a charcoal scoop-necked shift dress that came almost to my knees. I'd brought a pair of tall boots and two pairs of flats in red and navy, trying to keep to my two-bag limit. I slipped the red flats on and ran the flat iron through my hair to press the humidity out. My hair had become frizzy the moment I got off the airplane in New Orleans, and no amount of heat or product seemed to tame it for long.

A half hour later, Lucille was at the door. She looked healthier since I'd seen her at Christmas, with fuller cheeks and red highlights in her hair. Tonight she wore slim-cut jeans, a beat up brown motorcycle jacket and tall brown boots. Being back here was good for her, it seemed. That, along with being rid of that jackass Toph whom she'd been dating when I last saw her.

"Hey," she said, giving me a quick hug. "What's the dog emergency?"

In the living room, I heard the jingle of Bella's collar against the floor as she turned her head to look at us.

"I'll tell you on the way," I said.

"Is that what's you're wearing?" She tilted her head to the side.

"Yeah, why?"

She shrugged, stumbling over her words. "Awfully fancy," she said. "We're going to a place where you toss peanut shells on the floor."

"This is the most casual outfit I have."

"Seriously? Don't you have pants?"

"Yeah, that I wear out in the yard." I'd gotten so accustomed to business casual that I was uncomfortable around people if I wore most anything else. Khakis were for gardening. Jeans were for college kids.

"So put those on," she said.

"But I wear them in the yard."

She blinked at me.

"I'm starving, Lucille. Can we talk fashion later?"

She smiled and shrugged as we went outside and climbed into her tiny blue Volkswagen sedan.

Lucille drove us along the main road towards town and pulled over at a white clapboard building with a big front porch made from weathered lumber. Colored lights criss-crossed through the beams and a chalkboard outside proclaimed *Fresh Catch + Cold Beer.* The windows glowed with orange-tinted light.

"It doesn't look like much from the outside," Lucille said, "But it's my favorite. And they have fried green tomatoes."

Inside, it was all wood paneling and diner-style tables that were almost certainly from the 1950s. The chairs, mismatched, were a dozen different colors, all vinyl with aluminum and rivets. The bar was off to one side, with a jukebox and a pool table in the opposite corner. The place was half full, so we chose a booth in the back, near the jukebox. I'd never seen so much denim and plaid in my entire life.

A waitress came to take our orders, and Lucille greeted her by name. They chatted for a moment while I looked over the menu. Lucille finally caught my attention and said, "Want to split a seafood platter as big as our heads?"

"Only if it has fried green tomatoes," I said.

The waitress, Gina, grinned and nodded. "Anything to drink, girls?"

Lucille asked for a beer. I asked for a martini. Gina sauntered back to the bar.

"Everyone's looking at us," I said.

"They're trying to figure out who you are," Lucille said.

"Should I make an announcement? Would that stop the staring?"

She chuckled. "Word'll spread soon enough. This is basically the only place to hang out around here."

Gina came back with our drinks. My martini was in a lowball glass with an olive rolling around on the bottom like a marble. The glass was half full.

"I think she brought me a double," I said.

"See? Best place around."

"Cheers," I said and clinked my glass against hers.

"So what's new with you?" Lucille asked.

I told her about my meeting with Jeffrey, my job that was about to disappear. "They offered to bring me on as a part-time consultant, but I think I might hate that job anyway. So I'm taking this week to figure out if I just want to quit completely and start something new."

"Oh," she said.

"Enza thought a week away from the vortex might help me decide."

"It worked for me. Just took longer than a week."

"Are you still doing your master's program?"

"This is my last semester, so I'm down to thesis work and one class. I stay with a friend in Baton Rouge two or three nights a week."

"How's Buck?" I said.

"Much better." She smiled, like she'd almost put her past with Toph behind her. Enza had told me Lucille had stayed with her parents since the winter, helping her father recover from an accident. She was working on a master's in theater arts.

The jukebox whined an old Zeppelin song, the bass notes thrumming like a pulse. The crack of billiard balls split the air and a chorus of hoots erupted from the far corner. Lucille wiggled along with the music, sipping her beer and telling me about their spring play, a retelling of *The Tempest*.

On our second round, she said, "It was good to come back to something familiar for a while. You need that sometimes."

"I did the opposite," I said. "It's easier to make objective decisions if I step back a bit, you know?"

Lucille nodded. "Get away from the center of things."

"It felt like everything was falling apart. My job, my fiancé—but that's a whole 'nother long sad story about a cheating bastard."

Lucille frowned. "Well, you met my bastard. I don't know why I stayed with him for so long."

"Why do we stay? I think something in me is broken. Sometimes I think I just picked a bad match, but then I think it was my fault, too. I'm a workaholic. I know that."

"It's not your fault he cheated. I may be young, but I know that much is true."

I shrugged. "I drove him to it. I wasn't there enough for him."

"Nope," Lucille barked. "Not your fault. That's not how cheating works."

"Maybe."

"Not maybe," Lucille said, leaning closer.

"I like my lab, where everything's predictable. Ben was that in the beginning, but then one day he wasn't. And it wrecked everything."

She shrugged. "Unpredictable's not always bad. You'll find a better one, one who surprises you in the good way."

The music changed to something fast and Lucille pounded her fist on the table, making the glasses rattle. Then she stood up and said, "Come dance with me. I love this one."

"Everyone's already staring at me," I said. "I'm not going to make more of a spectacle of myself."

"Come on. Nobody in this place will dance with me because they're scared to death of Jack and my dad. And of Andre, of course. They all protect me so much I never have any fun." She stuck her lip out in a pout, tugging on my wrist. "Please," she whined.

"Maybe next time."

She groaned, staring up at the ceiling. Then she started dancing in a tiny circle, right next to me, raising her arms overhead, shaking her hips. "Fine," she said, exaggerating the movements. "I'll just be right here."

"Suit yourself." I sipped my martini as she twirled in her own bubble, letting the quizzical looks from the locals bounce off her like points of light from a disco ball. She wiggled against me, which seemed to just draw more attention to us, and I laughed in spite of myself.

"I see that foot tapping," she said. "Don't fight it."

When she shimmied to the side, the room narrowed to a point. And at the end of that point was Andre Dufresne, walking right toward us with just enough swagger to hold my attention. His badge, clipped to his belt, caught the light like a coin in a fountain and a flicker of surprise flashed over his face before he smiled. Andre, with the tiny wrinkles that showed around his eyes when he laughed his raucous laugh. He nodded a greeting, tilted his head to the side as he snuck up behind Lucille.

"Hey, Luce," he said, dropping his hand onto her shoulder. "Burning up the dance floor, I see."

She moonwalked past him and said, "I might have a partner if you didn't scare them all off with all that authority and whatnot. They all think you'll lock 'em up for touching me."

"And they're correct." He ruffled her hair like a big brother might. "I'll let you know when one of this lot's good enough for you."

"I can choose my own fellas, thank you," she said.

The song faded out and she took her seat at the table, winking at me. I took a long drink from the martini.

Andre turned to me and said, "Hi, Kate. I heard you were back in town." His hand rested on my shoulder for a moment, as if he wasn't sure if he should hug me.

"Dog-sitting," I said.

"Vacation," Lucille said, smoothing her hair back down. "Escaping the perils of the big city."

"Is that right?" he said. He'd rested one hand on his hip, one on the back of my chair. He smiled so his dimples showed. "It's good to see you again."

"You, too," I said, and something fluttered in my chest like a bird.

His eyes were greener than I remembered. His reddish hair was tousled, like he'd been driving all day with his windows down. It was just long enough to stand up in tufts, just a hint of curls. I bit my lip, thinking of how we'd sprawled out on the living room floor last Christmas, playing Scrabble and drinking bourbon way too far into the morning. I'd been staying with Enza, helping her survive the holiday collision of her old family with her new one, and out of nowhere Andre had appeared with his easy smile. I'd been completely smitten.

I'd also just broken up with Benjamin, so the timing of meeting Andre wasn't exactly great. We had chemistry, sure—but I don't do rebounds. They're selfish. I was a guest in my best friend's house, and the last thing I wanted to do was have a fling with her boyfriend's best friend and create more tension. Lord knows, Enza had enough drama in her life without adding me and my messed up love life to the mix.

So despite wishing I could tangle my fingers in the sheriff's hair and kiss him stupid that night last December, I'd gone back to my room upstairs and left him sleeping on the couch, Scrabble tiles littering the floor like confetti.

And now here he was, standing in a bar with no name, even more adorable than I remembered, staring at me like he was replaying every detail of that evening in his head.

"How long are you here?" he asked me.

Kate wiggled her eyebrows and I nudged her foot under the table.

"Just until Sunday," I said.

"Well maybe I'll see you around," he said.

"Maybe so."

"I certainly hope so."

Someone hollered to him from the bar and he tore his gaze away from me. He waved to Gina, who was holding a brown paper bag.

"Take out," he said. "Working late tonight."

"Ah, that's too bad," Lucille said. "Thought for sure you'd join us for the next dance."

"Rain check," he said, his eyes still fixed on mine. "You ladies get home safe tonight."

"Thanks, Andre," I said.

He turned back and said, "Good to see you again, Kate," and then strode towards the bar.

I watched him a little too long, his lean frame in the snug pants and shirt.

Lucille cleared her throat, then tapped the table in front of me.

"What?" I said.

She grinned and said in a voice one octave lower than her usual, "Good to see you again, Kate." She batted her eyelashes.

I snorted, feeling tipsy from the martini.

"He might be exactly what you need," Lucille said. "He could make you forget about all the perils of the city, all your work nonsense."

"Lucille!" I said. "He's like your brother."

She scoffed. "He needs a vacation, too. You two would be cute together."

"You've been hanging around with Enza too long."

She shrugged. "We gals have to look out for each other."

But I couldn't argue with her. It wasn't like the thought had never entered my mind.

And sat there in the far corner, percolating.

And resurfaced in dreams that left me breathless.

Chapter Three

THE NEXT DAY, I spent the morning doing exactly what Enza suggested. First I took a long walk up and down the gravel lane by the house. The little Victorian was situated on a few acres of tall grass and hay, encircled by dense cypress groves. A lagoon lay at the edge of the back yard, its bright water much more inviting than the brackish pools that lay in the swamp beyond. There were no neighboring houses that I could see. I walked along the tree line to clear my head, Bella never too far from my side. Then I laid out in the sun in a bikini and read a novel I'd had on my bedside table for a year. I'd brought my laptop outside, but refused to obsess over my email, checking it only once a day. I didn't want to see any messages from the lab, from my colleagues, and especially not from Jeffrey. It was unlikely, of course, that he would be communicating at all, but I couldn't handle seeing his email signature right now, that ridiculous red script that was two point sizes too big. It was possible some colleagues would reach out in a kind way, maybe even with leads on other jobs, but I didn't want to hear their concern at the moment.

It was tempting to start searching for new jobs, but reading the postings was exhausting. I'd been promoted last year, and at first had been pleased with the prospect of more job security. The lab had consistency. My projects changed, but my objectives stayed the same. I looked for cellular patterns, growth and decay. It was soothing. Not at all like the other aspects of my life, which seemed to have zero predictability. Surprises made me nervous. I preferred being presented with options and having time to prepare myself, weigh potential outcomes, and then make my decision. Spontaneity left me too little time to prepare.

I'd moved one of Enza's lawn chairs down to the dock at the lagoon. The water was a warm greenish-blue, but I still imagined it as a prehistoric pond full of alligators, all waiting to bite my limbs off. Enza told me she went swimming all the time, but I couldn't bring myself to even dangle my feet in. Now, Bella was stretched out beside me on the dock, apparently still full of equal parts lasagna and regret.

Across the yard, the breeze shook the bottles that hung in the big oak tree behind the house. The oldest bottles had turned amethyst, but the newer ones were pale green and amber. Enza's grandmother had begun hanging them decades ago, to ward off trickster spirits, she said. Enza had started adding her own to continue the tradition, and since she said there was no shortage of mischievous spirits around here. The wind whistled over the mouths of the bottles, and though it had sounded spooky at first, it now soothed me like wind chimes.

As I turned back to my novel, the dog scrambled to her feet and stared towards the house, her bobbed tail wagging. A car door slammed and she rushed toward the porch, barking all the way.

I grabbed Enza's bathrobe that I'd borrowed and quickly wrapped it around me, then fumbled to get my sneakers on. It must have been Lucille, I thought, and walked up to the house.

But instead of Lucille's little blue Volkswagen, there was a Jeep Cherokee marked *Sheriff*. Andre stepped around the side of the porch, the dog dancing in a circle around him.

I gasped and cinched the robe tighter around me.

"Hey, Kate," he said. "How are you?"

"Sheriff Dufresne," I said, crossing my arms over my chest, wishing the robe was full length.

He grinned a crooked grin and scratched Bella's ears as she put her front paws above his knee. "So formal," he said, fixing his eyes on mine. His dimples showed when he smiled, and I felt my ears tingling with his pleasant drawl.

"You're in uniform," I said. "I feel like I can't call you Andre unless you're in normal clothes."

He glanced down, as if he'd forgotten what he'd been wearing.

"What are you doing here?" I asked.

"Oh, you know. Just wanted to say hi."

"So you drove over? Most people just use the telephone to do that."

"I was in the neighborhood," he said with a shrug. "Had a call out this way."

I bit my lip, forcing back a smile. "So you just dropped by, without calling first? The last time you did that, you found me naked. Or did you forget about that?" That had been Christmas, when he startled me so bad I thought he was a burglar. I'd thrown my hair dryer at him and left a cut on his eyebrow. Why did everyone around here just pop by unannounced? I was constantly amazed by the casual nature down here, and found it hard to get used to.

"No ma'am," he said, tugging briefly at his collar. "That would be difficult to forget."

I loved the way he blushed, how the pink started on his cheeks and spread down to his neckline. It made his eyes look greener.

"That lick with the blow-dryer could have affected your memory," I said.

"I had every intention of knocking loudly," he said, holding his hands up by his sides. "Last time, I thought I was walking into an empty house. This time, I know the circumstances." There was that wry grin again, the kind that hinted he wasn't always buttoned down and by the book.

Bella plopped down at his feet, fixing her narrowed eyes on me. It was clear where her loyalty lay.

"Well, come inside if you like," I said. "I can be more hospitable indoors, with tea. Don't y'all do that down here?"

"I don't want to interrupt your outdoor time," he said, gesturing toward the robe. "I just realized that I left last night without saying the most important thing."

"Oh?"

"Yeah. I forgot to say that you can call me if you should need anything. I just live a few minutes from here." He pulled a business card from his shirt pocket and handed it to me. "My cell number's on the back."

"In case of emergency?" I said.

It was a friendly gesture, but the way he was looking at me was more than just friendly. He'd looked at me like that in December, on the night of the Scrabble game, after he'd beat me by fifty points and then kissed me until I thought my heart would hammer a hole in my chest.

"I should get going," he said. "I'm on the clock." He gave Bella a final pat on the head, ruffling her fur.

"Thanks, Andre." I tucked the card into the top of my swimsuit.

His eyes followed my fingers and then darted back to my face. "See you, Kate."

Most of the time, my name sounded clipped, like a quick cut in the air. But when Andre said, *Kate,* with that musical lilt, it was as if his tongue savored the word like it would a top-shelf bourbon. I thought of the way he'd whispered it that night as his lips brushed over my ear. My skin tingled at the memory of his hands sliding along my arms, my shoulders. If Enza hadn't been asleep in the next room, I probably would have let him kiss me all over, let my name roll off his tongue until dawn.

He started to walk away, then turned back. "You want to grab dinner one night?" he said. "Catch up?"

"Sure," I said, trying to match his casual tone. "Sounds nice."

He smiled and walked back to his car, as slow as a river, and I knew that if I was alone with him, it would most certainly make my moral compass spin until it caught fire. But I was starting to believe that my friends were right: I should stop overthinking, live in the moment. Do things that made me happy.

Bella sat down next to me and snorted.

"This is about to get a lot more complicated, isn't it?" I said. "Why'd you go and let me do that? You're supposed to be a watchdog, you know, keeping me out of trouble."

Her pink mouth opened into a yawn and she shook her head so hard her collar jingled.

"Traitor," I said, but this sort of trouble might be just the thing I needed.

LUCILLE CALLED AN HOUR LATER. "Want to go out tonight?"

"We just went out last night."

"So?" she said, and after a pause, "What else do you have to do around here? Do you really want to sit on the couch with a dog all night? That's not a vacation."

"Okay. What time?"

"I'll come pick you up at six," Lucille said.

"I can just meet you there."

"No, no. We have some work to do first."

She hung up before I could ask her to elaborate.

Bella was still wandering around outside when Lucille arrived, making her mysterious rounds through the swamp. There was no telling what her daily dog business entailed, but apparently, she sometimes came home muddy and had to be hosed off before she could come inside the house. Enza had left a small inflatable pool in the back yard that could be used for these emergencies, but thankfully it had not come to this. Yet.

Lucille knocked on the door carrying two brightly patterned tote bags in green and yellow.

"What's all that?" I said.

"We have to get you appropriate attire."

She nudged past me and emptied the contents of the tote bags on the sofa in the living room. She held two shirts up to my chest, frowning and tossing one aside.

"Try this one," she said, and thrust a pair of jeans at me as well. "We're about the same size."

"Um," I sputtered, but she was already steering me toward Enza's room down the hall. "Go change. I'll get the rest ready."

In Enza's room, I took off my khaki pants and button-down blouse and squeezed myself into the jeans. They were a dark wash with a few small threadbare patches on the thighs, like college students wear. The thin blouse was off-white with a lacy upper part that I could see straight through. It reminded me of the tiny crocheted snowflake ornaments my grandmother used to make. Cut on the bias, it fell lower on one hip than the other.

When I walked into the living room, Lucille actually squealed. "That's so much better!" she sang. "You look like a real girl."

"I look like I've been chewed by an animal."

"You look like you know how to have fun. Or at the very least, locate it."

"I'm not sure I can sit in these," I said, attempting a squat.

"We won't be doing much sitting if I have anything to say about it." She thrust a pair of square-toed cowboy boots into my hands. "Your dancing shoes," she said.

"Are we going to a rodeo?"

"What size are you?"

"Nine."

"Those should work."

I rolled my eyes and pulled the boots on. They were comfortable, and their heels made a clacking sound that wasn't entirely unpleasant. I liked a heel that announced my presence.

"Okay, now about your hair," Lucille said.

"What's wrong with my hair?"

"Honey, you're in Louisiana. Using a flat iron will only

bring you frizz and heartache." She pulled a spray bottle out of the green tote back and walked behind me, spritzing my hair with what I assumed was water. She scrunched and fluffed and applied a little gel to soften the resulting curls, then stepped back and smiled.

"I smell like a piña colada, Lucille."

"And you look stunning."

I sighed and walked to the mirror in the hallway, the boot heels clacking like hooves.

My hair hung in soft waves, like I'd been out at the beach with just enough breeze. With the new clothes, I didn't look much like myself, but the look wasn't bad. At least I'd blend in this way and wouldn't be gawked at by strangers all night.

"Okay," Lucille said. "Let's roll."

At the bar, which I'd learned everyone just called "The Last Stop," Lucille and I ordered burgers to fortify ourselves before moving on to tequila shots.

"This'll loosen you up," she said. "You need to relax and have some fun."

"That seems to be the consensus."

She wasn't wrong. When we'd met last Christmas, we'd both had the misfortune of being with men that were all wrong for us. Lucille's situation had been far worse than mine, but she was doing well now. She'd adapted, readjusted, and it made me think I was in need of serious readjustment myself. I'd defined myself by my work for too long, and it was likely Benjamin was a casualty of that. He might have been a jerk, but he was still a wake-up call.

When I looked at Lucille, I saw a chance to make myself over in a way that mattered much more than just blending in to the local scene with a more natural appearance. Regrouping would be good for me, help me figure out what my "natural" really was.

After waiting the requisite half hour after eating (it was like swimming, Lucille told me—you have to wait or you get a cramp), Lucille pulled me to my feet and the tequila took over and then we were dancing in between the tables by the jukebox. Everyone was watching.

And I didn't care.

Lucille grabbed my hands and twirled me around, our boot heels pounding the floor boards just a little out of rhythm to a twangy song I didn't recognize. Lucille was a dervish, full of light. The air around her shimmered. It felt good to laugh as I mirrored her moves, trying to keep up with her. She spun me around again and when she did, I caught sight of Andre across the room. He was leaning against a barstool, his elbow propped on the bar, staring at us with his lips parted. When he caught me looking, he smiled and raised his hand up in a half-wave, like he'd just happened to glance in our direction.

The music changed to something slow and Lucille followed my gaze to the other side of the room. Andre walked over to us, carrying another bag of take-out in the crook of his arm. He looked bewildered, like he'd just witnessed something and he had no idea how to write it up in his report.

"Hey you two," he said. "Another girls' night out?" He was apparently off-duty now, wearing his dark brown uniform pants with a white tee shirt and no duty belt. He'd skipped his shave for a couple of days, judging by the dark shadow of stubble on his face.

"Hey," Lucille said. "You're right in time for the next round."

"So I see." His eyes rested on mine.

I eased into the booth and Lucille plopped down into the opposite side. She pretended to be oblivious, staying close to the edge so Andre couldn't sit next to her. I slid over to make room for him and he sat, his thigh brushing against mine.

Lucille grinned like a cat.

"Care to join us?" I said. "Lucille's giving dance lessons."

"I was just on my way home," he said. "Dinner to go."

Lucille frowned. "Have it here with us. You want a beer? I'll go get a pitcher." She was up before he could protest.

"I think she wants you to stay," I said.

He smiled. "How about you?"

I did want him to stay. And I wanted to feel his scratchy cheek against my shoulder, feel the warmth of his hands, the beating of his heart. I wanted Lucille to be right, that he needed a vacation that included me. I knew our relationship couldn't extend beyond this tiny town, but I was starting to think I might be okay with that. He was nice, he was fun, and he was good to me—I needed all of that right now.

We could do this, right? No one would be hurt if we managed our expectations.

"Of course," I said. "Join us."

He opened the bag and pulled out a wrapped burger and a small paper tray heaped with fries. Lucille came back with a pitcher of beer and three glasses. She poured us all beers, then took a sip of her own before going back to the jukebox. Instead of scooting around to her side of the booth, Andre stayed right where he was, by my side, his thigh barely touching mine. He was so close I could smell a hint of a musky cologne, and I caught myself leaning closer.

"Want some fries?" he said, sipping his beer.

I popped one into my mouth. "Thanks."

He said, "You look nice. Different."

"Wow. Thanks," I said, teasing him. "Just for that, I'll eat all your fries."

He smiled. "No, I mean you look relaxed. Like you're enjoying yourself."

"Lucille's determined to make sure of that."

He glanced toward the corner, where Lucille was back to dancing in her tiny circle. She was right: the men around her kept stealing glances, but none would approach. My older brothers had been the same way when I was growing up, scaring the daylights out of any boy who ventured too close to me. It drove me crazy, but part of me liked feeling protected by them. It wasn't that they made me feel fragile; rather, they made me feel rare and valued. No one had made me feel that since then. Lucille was lucky.

Andre leaned closer to talk to me over the music. He watched my eyes when he spoke, and he made dorky jokes to make me laugh. Despite feeling more at ease with him than I had with anyone in a long time, including Benjamin, it was hard to imagine our thing going anywhere. Benjamin and I had looked good on paper: we had similar upbringings, we were both logical people who spent most of our lives in analysis mode. We were fiscally responsible with matching 401(K)s. We discussed options thoroughly and didn't make snap decisions. We were alike in more ways than we were different, and I thought that meant we were well-suited enough to last a few decades.

But I had been wrong.

So if I couldn't make it work with someone like Ben, someone who looked so right for me on paper, how could I hope to make it work with someone like Andre, who was so very different from me?

The tequila had made me bold, and this fearless voice was rising like a tidal wave, screaming at me to stop thinking long-term. Perhaps I needed someone like Andre to just recalibrate my brain.

If he could recalibrate my body—well, that could be fun, too.

I imagined pushing the fries out of the way, leaning over and kissing him right on the mouth in front of everyone, telling him to take me home with him when he turned to look at me.

I froze like a rabbit.

"What are you doing tomorrow night?" he said.

I shook my head, mostly to knock loose those thoughts of kissing him and climbing into his lap. "Probably the same thing we're doing tonight," I said. "Lucille tells me there's not a lot to do around here."

He finished his beer. "You could spend the night with me, instead."

I coughed and for a minute thought beer would come right out my nose.

He laughed, turning red around the collar. "I mean, spend the evening. Go to dinner. Better yet, let me cook you dinner and we can get out of this dive."

"Dive?"

His eyebrow arched. "I love this place, but it's a dive." Hoots of laughter erupted from the far corner and he nodded towards the group of guys shooting pool. "What do you say?"

"Okay." His house, I thought. That was good. I could leave when I was ready, and not feel like I had to kick him out.

He smiled. "Great. Seven o'clock okay?"

"Sure," I said. What was happening to me? Why could I only manage one word at a time?

"Let me write down the address for you." He pulled a pen and notepad from his pants pocket and scribbled down his address. Over by the jukebox, a tall guy with a military-style haircut had wandered into Lucille's orbit, dancing close. Andre glanced in her direction, but turned back to me.

"Okay," I said. "I'll see you tomorrow."

He leaned closer, like he was about to divulge a secret. "I'm sorry," he said, his fingers brushing over my arm. "But I have the early shift tomorrow."

"Oh." The word whooshed out like I'd been punched. I resisted the urge to lay my hand on his arm and pull him back into the booth.

He stood, leaving a cold space next to me where his warmth had been.

"Y'all enjoy the rest of your evening," he said. His crooked smile said he didn't want to leave, either. His eyes lingered on me for a moment, and then he was striding towards Lucille, whose face fell when she saw him approach. Andre gave the young guy the once-over, the tilt of his head a clear signal I could read from even thirty feet away. The young man's shoulders sagged ever so slightly as he shook Andre's hand. The young man smiled at Lucille and then walked back to a table where his buddies sat with a pitcher. Andre slapped Lucille on the shoulder and then strode toward the front door, nodding towards me as he passed.

Lucille, frowning, stomped back to the table. "Did you see that? It never fails."

"He's just looking out for you, Luce."

"He told me to call if we needed a ride home."

"That was nice of him."

She refilled her glass and said, "After he introduced himself as Sheriff Dufresne and sent Eric headed for the hills."

"Who's Eric?"

"I guess we'll never know." She sipped her beer and said, "He's got moves, that sheriff. Serious moves."

She wasn't wrong about that, either.

"Come on," she said. "Let's go dance ourselves sober."

LATER THAT NIGHT, when the tequila had worn off and my pajamas were on, I stretched out on the couch in the living room and put on a movie—some monster flick from the 1970s with a radioactive reptile. I had a weakness for old monster movies, their villainous creatures born of lab accidents and meteorites. Their depictions of scientists were almost as hilarious as the monsters themselves.

After going over the evening again and again, lingering on the thought of Andre's stubbly beard tickling my skin, I texted Enza. *Andre asked me over for dinner.*

No response.

I said yes. Thoughts?

No answer. Where was she? Bella skulked into the living room and sat on her haunches, staring at me. I'd made a pizza when I came home, and she was miffed because she hadn't been offered a nibble.

"This could just be friendly dinner, right? He might not think it's a thing."

Her eyes narrowed.

"You're right. He doesn't think it's just friendly. I don't think either of us want just friendly. That's okay, right?"

She cocked her head to the side.

"Maybe we both need the thing. That's okay, too. We're adults. We like each other. We have fun together."

When half the pizza was gone and the savage alien reptile had been vanquished, Enza still hadn't answered me. Bella followed me into the kitchen and watched as I put the rest of the pizza in the fridge, no doubt hoping I'd drop part of it.

When I went upstairs to bed, I lay there for a long time listening to the wind rattle the bottles in the oak tree. It was a melody that invited memories of ghosts and spirits, eerie in the darkness. For the first time all week, I wasn't thinking about work, replaying that last day at the lab in my mind.

Instead, I was thinking of Andre, how my name sounded on his lips, how his lips had felt against my neck, and how badly I wanted to feel that again with him, despite the fact that I'd only feel it for a few more days.

It was impossible to forget those things. They were a constant I couldn't ignore.

Chapter Four

THE WHINING outside my bedroom door was persistent, punctuated by the clatter of claws on hardwood. When I pulled the sheet over my head, the noise turned to sharp little yips that reverberated through the plaster walls. Enza had warned me that Bella would wake me if I wasn't up early enough for her liking, but I hadn't expected such a dramatic display.

When the barks became louder, I rolled out of bed and opened the door. The dog darted into the room and stood behind me, pressing her wet nose against the back of my calf.

"Don't be bossy," I said. "I understand this is in your genetic code, but you need to adapt. Not every creature is a herd animal."

She huffed. Bella liked her herd to behave.

I plucked my cell phone from the night stand, anxious to see what Enza thought of my dinner with Andre. Even though she teased me about seeing him, part of me worried that she'd be hurt if our relationship didn't extend beyond the end of this week. Enza didn't think much of flings, either. She was a hopeless romantic and was no doubt hoping Andre would be my dashing knight on a big white horse.

I, however, didn't believe in knights and their steadfast white horses. Sometimes I thought I was the opposite of romantic. Ergo, Benjamin.

It was almost quarter till nine, and the room was already bright with morning sunlight. Enza had repainted this room a buttercream color, like something she'd seen in a magazine. It had original hardwood floors, high ceilings and tall windows painted white. This had once been Enza's grandmother's bedroom, but now she called it Kate's Room, no doubt hoping that would make me comfortable enough to visit more often. I'd never been to this part of Louisiana before Enza came here, and though I teased her about the cat-sized mosquitoes and the Godzillas lurking in the swamp, I could see why she'd stayed. The air was crisp, filled with chirping birds and the scent of magnolia. Colors seemed brighter, from the blossoming trees to the lush green of the grass, and the sky felt wide with wonder. The world in general was more vibrant here, more alive. Raleigh was more gray to me with each passing day, with its grid of pavement and sidewalks, shades of charcoal and ash punctuated by spots of pink from the occasional azalea or tulip tree. This seemed like sheer wilderness, full of mystery and possibilities. I inhaled the sweetness of the air, hoping it might transform me from the inside out.

Bella barked once, then bounded out into the hall and down the stairs.

"All right, all right," I said. "I'm coming." I wrapped my bathrobe around me and plodded down the stairs to make coffee. Bella stood by the front door, looking first at the doorknob, then at me, then back to the door when I didn't move fast enough.

When I unlocked the door and opened the screen, she raced out and paused for a brief moment, sniffing the air, as if waiting for a signal. When she got it, her ears flattened and she took off in the direction of the lagoon, streaking through the grass like a greyhound.

This was the routine, Enza had told me. Bella liked to romp around outside all day, sometimes not returning until after sundown. She spent her nights inside the house on guard duty. Jack rarely left her out at night: not because he was afraid for her, but because the dog preferred to be inside with him. Bella, like all herding dogs, liked to know her flock was safe. As long as I was staying here, I was her flock (though the lasagna incident seemed to say she felt otherwise). Jack had warned me that if I left her out at night, she would whine and bark until I let her in. If that didn't work, she'd shove the screen door with her paw, banging it against the doorframe in a racket that would insure compliance.

"She's stubborn as hell," Jack had said. "But she'll keep you safe."

And that much was certainly true: Enza had eventually told me over a bottle of wine that Bella had saved her skin a few times, alerting her to both an intruder and a house fire. It was hard to hold a grudge against a dog like that.

I stumbled into the kitchen and started the coffee, then cracked a couple of eggs in a skillet. My phone blinked with a text message from Enza.

Go for it, she wrote. *It's just dinner. Have fun.*

A few minutes later, she'd sent another one: *If it doesn't work out, it doesn't work out. We're all adults here. Give yourself a break.*

Of course she would say that. She had a new appreciation for risk-taking, ever since she met Jack. He'd won her over with his easy charm, something that seemed standard-issue in these parts. Ninety-five percent of my body was saying, *Relax, have fun and see where this goes,* but I couldn't shake the five percent of myself that persisted with its warning: *Stop, before you do something that can't be undone, before you let him get close enough to hurt you.*

LUCILLE TALKED me into spending the afternoon in New Orleans, shopping for a few outfits that were less, as she said, "business-boring."

"You can't wear a button-down shirt on a hot date," she said, gesturing toward the pinstriped blouse I was wearing. "You need something that makes him want to tear it off with his teeth."

She led me from one boutique to the next, tossing blouses and jeans over her arm, pointing to mannequins when I questioned her pairings. She flitted from one rack to another, teasing out bright colors and patterns like the hosts on those television makeover shows. She sent me to the dressing room with a pile of clothes, demanding to see every outfit.

After an exhausting three hours, I had four new tops that exposed my collarbones, two pairs of jeans that were slim-cut, and a red print wrap dress that Lucille had deemed appropriate for any dinner that might involve wine. "If Marilyn Monroe was going to go out in a row boat on an idyllic afternoon, this is what she would wear," Lucille said. "Look, it even works with boots."

We stopped to recharge at a little coffee shop across the street from the last boutique. Already it was sweltering outside, so I was grateful for an air-conditioned cafe with strong coffee.

"What's the matter?" Lucille said after a while. "You're pushing your cheesecake around in circles."

I shrugged. "Maybe I shouldn't do this, not with Andre. I'm only here for a few days. Maybe I should just keep it friendly."

She sighed, sipping her coffee. "You're overthinking."

I snorted. "It's sort of what I'm trained to do."

"Don't worry so much. It's just dinner."

But we both knew that wasn't entirely true.

"But what happens if this goes bad?" I said. "What if I hurt him, and then Jack hates me, and you hate me, and Enza hates me?"

"Nobody's going to hate you," she said. "People come together, and sometimes they fall apart. But you have to take chances."

"How'd you get so wise?"

She ate the last bite of her cake and said. "I read a lot of Shakespeare."

I laughed. "I remember Shakespeare being one disaster after another."

"There's a lot to be learned from disaster."

I sighed, sipping my coffee.

"Look," she said. "Do you like Andre?"

"Of course."

"And it's obvious he likes you. So give yourself this week to see what happens. You could do a hell of a lot worse than him, you know." She stared at me for a long moment, then said, "You do experiments for a living, right?"

"Yes."

"Okay then. This is an experiment. But you need to quit all this over-analyzing."

"Enza tells me the same thing. She says I treat the world like it's a lab." Truth be told, I envied Enza's ability to seek out wonder and surprises. For her, it was a reflex.

"Labs have a certain predictability," she said. "I get that. So do stage plays. But the delight happens in the surprise, right? The unscripted."

She dug through her purse and pulled out a rubber band. Then she reached for my hand and put the rubber band on my wrist like a bracelet.

"What's that for?" I said.

"You need to break a bad habit. This is how I quit smoking."

Before I could question her, she popped the band against my skin.

"Ow!"

"Every time you start overthinking this thing with Andre, you do that," she said. "Re-train your brain. Just enjoy the moment and see where it takes you. My guess is that you could use a little unpredictability."

I stared at her, but couldn't argue.

"Let yourself be open to surprises," she said. "You might find out you like them."

I could do this. I'd done a week-long juice cleanse, for chrissakes. If I could go a whole week drinking nothing but grapefruit juice and god-awful grass-flavored smoothies, I could change the way I felt about unplanned events.

"Okay," I said. "For one week, I will embrace surprises."

"And not try to calculate the outcome of every move you make."

"Yes," I said.

She made me shake on it, then clinked her tiny coffee cup against mine. "Just wait," she said. "This is going to be the best week of your life."

By the time I got back to Enza's house, it was nearly six o'clock. I'd agreed to meet Andre at seven. He only lived about ten minutes away, down the main road and across a canal. My day outside had left my clothes sweaty and my hair tangled. After a quick shower, I let my hair air dry while I dressed, hoping to tame it the way Lucille had. I slipped into a new pair of jeans and a boat-necked tee shirt. After a little mascara, lipstick, and enough paste to keep the frizz from my wavy hair, I was done. My skin seemed luminous for a change, my eyes brighter blue. Humidity might not be so bad for me after all.

While out with Lucille, I'd forgotten to pick up something to take to Andre's. It was rude to show up empty-handed, especially since he was cooking dinner himself. There was no time to stop anywhere on the way, so I dug through Enza's cupboard until I found a sealed bottle of rye bourbon with an orange vintage-looking label. It was the same kind we'd had during the Scrabble game that changed everything.

I called Bella from the porch, but she didn't show. Typical, I thought. She was getting back at me for not letting her out early enough this morning. The wind was picking up, howling along the lips of the bottles in the trees. The leaves of the oaks and walnuts trembled, upturned so their pale undersides gleamed. It was a sure sign that a storm was coming, as certain as the clouds that gathered from the west, darkening the sky to periwinkle. That kind of sky meant trouble was coming, fast and sure of its course.

Chapter Five

ANDRE'S HOUSE was a single story river-style, set back in a grove of oaks. White with wood shingles, it had dark blue shutters that opened from the bottom to fan open like gills. It was close enough to the canal that I could smell the brine of the dark water as I walked up onto the porch. Wrens twittered in the trees, fussing from one of the hedges as they guarded nests barely visible though the spring leaves. The air felt heavy with approaching rain, the sun grapefruit pink as it dipped towards the tree line in the darkening sky.

After I rang the doorbell, I heard a muffled reply from inside. The door opened and there was Andre, his blue plaid shirt dusted in flour. One distinct white handprint lay on his thigh, crisp against the dark of denim. He held a wooden spoon in one hand, a floppy red oven mitt on the other.

"Hi, Kate," he said, my name lingering on his tongue. "Come on in."

"Hi." I thrust the bottle towards him and said, "I hope it's ok to bring the sheriff bourbon."

His fingers brushed over mine as he took it. "That's my favorite."

I followed him inside. "Not that I'm saying we should finish that whole bottle tonight."

He smiled so the wrinkles at the corners of his eyes showed. "Copy that. We'll take our time and finish it slow." As he led me down the hall to the kitchen, my eyes drifted from his shoulders to his hips, and I wondered exactly what he meant by that. I caught myself considering multiple scenarios and then snapped the rubber band on my wrist.

Stop thinking ahead, Kate. Stop calculating.

Instead, I concentrated on the sway of his shoulders, his slow, easy walk. He was tall and svelte, a little over six feet, and made a room more comfortable just by being in it. His sleeves were rolled up to his elbows, his shirt neatly tucked into snug jeans.

"Hey," he said, and I felt my cheeks burn, certain he'd caught me staring. "You like shrimp, right?"

"You bet," I said. "I never get it back home. I have this rule about eating seafood more than fifty miles inland."

He nodded. "Not a bad rule."

If heaven had a smell, it would be Andre's kitchen. Butter, garlic, the brine of the ocean, herbs too magical to identify. I closed my eyes for a second, just to take it all in, and realized I was licking my lips. When I opened my eyes, Andre was watching me, arms crossed, grinning a wicked grin.

"I miss this," I said, feeling myself blush.

"Seafood?" he said.

I nodded. "That, too," I said under my breath.

He stirred something in a skillet on the stove top and then removed a casserole dish that looked a lot like étouffée with shrimp on top. His kitchen was small, but had a couple of windows that he'd opened to let in the breeze. There was a dining table against the wall with three chairs, Shaker style. The walls were off-white, the cabinets painted to match. It was warm, intimate.

"How about a glass of wine to start?" he said. He held two glasses in one hand, a bottle of white in the other.

"Sounds great," I said.

He poured two glasses and handed me one. "Welcome back, Kate. The bayou missed you."

I clinked my glass against his and sipped. He set an array of dishes on the table—sausages, shrimp étouffée, green beans in garlic sauce—and paused as he leaned down and saw the dusting of flour on his shirt and pants. He stepped back toward the sink and brushed his hands over the fabric. "Seems I always make a mess," he said.

"Not at all. This is dedication," I said, reaching for the spoon in the rice. "I'm going to try to be ladylike here, even though I'm starving."

He laughed. "Don't hold back on my account. You do what you have to do."

I grinned and spooned a little of everything onto my plate. "How was your day of sheriffing?" I said, and it sounded simultaneously like the most asinine question ever, and also the most natural, as if I had spent the last hundred evenings asking him.

He bit a shrimp in half and said, "There was a lot of boring paperwork, a noise complaint, a huge delivery of girl scout cookies, and an alligator that rang a woman's doorbell and had to be removed."

"Seriously? Now I have to worry about alligators slithering up to my door?"

"They waddle, really, until they get up some speed. But this woman out by Bayou Gris was just minding her business, fixing her kids lunch or whatever, and heard the doorbell ring. She was slow to answer, and the bell rang over and over, impatient-like."

I laughed, reaching for my wine. "You're making this up."

"No," he said, holding his hands up, palms toward me. "I swear. So the woman goes to answer the door, pissed that this person is so rude, ready to curse him to pieces, and flings the door open to find a six-foot gator on her stoop, his snout pressed against the doorbell."

I snorted. "What does one do with a rude alligator?"

He shrugged, sipping his wine. "Make a killer pair of boots."

"You're joking."

"We hauled him down to the refuge south of here. They take strays."

"I think that's the weirdest thing you could have told me."

He laughed, dragging his fingers along his stubbled jaw. I imagined his rough cheek sliding along my shoulder, laughing that throaty laugh in my ear, and I wished the breeze would pick up to cool the room off before I completely lost my mind.

"Nah," he said. "Things around here get way weirder than that." He speared another shrimp with his fork and said, "How are you making out at Enza and Jack's?"

"Okay," I said, trying to eat slowly. After too many years of short lunch breaks, I tended to eat like someone was about to take my food away. "It's nice out there, but the dog has it in for me."

He grinned. "She can be a handful, all right."

"My first night, I went up to take a bath and she tore into

the lasagna I left out to cool. She wrecked the kitchen, and then she barfed in my brand new tote bag."

"That's terrible," he said. "Lasagna's my favorite. I can never make it right."

I shook my head. "That bag was vintage Anne Klein. I'd had it less than a week and had to throw it away."

"That bad, huh?"

"Oh, she thoroughly ruined it. You can't get vomit out of silk lining."

He winced, pushing his food around the plate. Thunder rumbled in the distance.

"Sorry. Not proper dinner conversation."

"Oh no," he said. "I've heard worse over dinner."

I smiled. "Worse than revenge barfing? Let's hear it."

He waved me off, pouring more wine for both of us. "Later," he said. "I can't tell you all my best stuff right up front."

"Afraid we'll run out of things to talk about?"

His eyes rested on mine. "I have to give you a reason to come back, right?"

By the time we finished the bottle of wine, we'd moved to the living room. The storm had rolled right over us, lightning crashing outside, rain slapping against the windows. Andre had lit a few candles on the coffee table, expecting the power to go out as the storm gathered strength. So far the lights had only flickered, but he'd turned most of them out, leaving just one lamp on the in the corner. We were on his sofa, where he seemed to be making a concerted effort not to encroach onto my cushion. He'd poured us each a bourbon with a couple of ice cubes, but mine sat untouched on the coffee table. He sipped his, slowly.

"After you left in December, I wasn't sure I'd see you again." His eyes were fixed on mine, wide in the dim light.

"I'd have come back eventually. Enza's here."

"Yeah, but still." He raked his fingers through his hair, making it stand up in the most delightful way. "I guess I was hoping I wouldn't just see you around when you were visiting Enza."

I tugged at the rubber band on my wrist, trying to simply listen, and not to think too hard about what that might mean. After a few moments of silence, I said, "I'm glad you asked me over, Andre."

His eyes brightened at the sound of his name. "I'm glad you said yes," he said, "but I'm sorry about your job."

I started. "How'd you know about that?"

He shrugged. "Small towns have no secrets."

"Lucille."

Thunder rumbled in the distance, the air vibrating between us. "You'll find a better job," he said. "Someone as talented as you."

I felt a blush rising in my cheeks, thinking of the sorts of talent he might be hiding.

He grinned his crooked grin and said, "You should move down here."

I swallowed hard, snapped the rubber band on my wrist.

"What's that?" he said.

"Ah, nothing." I reached for my bourbon, tucked the wrist with the rubber band under my opposite elbow.

He smiled at me, curious, reaching for my hand. The warmth of his fingers made my heart skip like a record.

"It's silly," I said. "Just a way to break a habit, like biting your nails."

"You bite your nails?"

"No." I relented and held out my wrist so he could see the tan rubber band, camouflaged by a couple of silver bangles. I took a big sip of the bourbon and felt its pleasant sting in the back of my throat. His hand felt solid, holding mine. "It's aversive conditioning. When you do the thing you're trying not to do, you snap the rubber band so you associate the thing you're trying not to do with pain."

"What is it you're trying not to do?"

Ruin this by overthinking. Miss out on someone like you. Crush your heart and mine.

"I'm trying to make myself open to unpredictability," I said.

He raised his eyebrows.

"It sounds silly, I know. But I've always hated surprises. And Enza keeps telling me I'm sabotaging myself by overthinking everything and rejecting surprises. So this week I'm re-training myself and staying open to the unpredictable. I snap this every time I overthink." I snapped the band for emphasis.

"I make you overthink things?"

"You were sort of a surprise."

"And you hate surprises," he said.

"I *used to* hate surprises. For me, surprises meant catastrophe. Not delight. Surprises meant things like a grandfather dying, my parents getting divorced, getting fired, my fiancé cheating on me."

He looked sad, his brow furrowed. "I'm sorry. Everybody should have nice surprises."

I shrugged. "You're turning out to be all right."

His laughter filled the room and made my skin tingle. "I'll take that," he said, then sat up straighter and placed his hand over his chest as if taking an oath. "Kate McDonnell, I will do my best not to be a catastrophe."

I swatted his hand away, blushing. "I said that all wrong. I blame the bourbon."

He smiled, leaning closer, crossing onto my cushion. "Nothing wrong with laying down some ground rules." He propped his elbow on the back of the sofa, resting his head against his hand. "You got any others?"

For a moment his gaze held me fast between what was and what could be, and I felt pulled to him, as if by a taut rope. Before I could convince myself not to, I leaned over and kissed him. His body tensed, and in the next moment he was pulling me onto his lap, tangling his hand in my hair. The room tilted with the softness of his lips, the hard edge of his teeth. His stubbled cheek scratched my neck and I moved closer, straddling him. My pulse hammered in my head, louder than the rain outside, and his hands tightened against my hips.

He pulled away, leaning his head back against the sofa to gaze up at me. His chest rose and fell beneath my hands as he said, "That really wasn't the response I was expecting."

"Should I not have done that?" I moved to slide off his lap, but he caught me fast.

"I've been hoping you'd do that since the minute you walked in," he said, his hands squeezing my thighs. "I'd really like you to do it again."

I grinned, leaning down to kiss him again, softer this time. Outside, the wind picked up and tree limbs scratched against the window behind us.

When I let him go, he said, "I'd also really like you to stay the night."

"As opposed to leaving now, during the storm of the century?"

He smiled. "Ah, this is nothing. The big storm's coming in the next day or two. Tropical depression is skirting right past us. This is just the edge of it."

"Guess I can forget working on my tan."

"Just for the next couple of days," he said, and his eyes drifted over me as if he were deciding where the tan lines might fall. He slid his thumb along my collar bone, and I wasn't going anywhere.

Thunder rattled the windows again and I flinched at the sound.

"Don't worry," he said, his lips against the hollow of my throat. "I'll keep you warm."

He was all taut muscle and tight grip, sleepy eyes and rumpled hair, and I felt like a bird being swept into a hurricane. I leaned into him and caught his hair in my fingers, tugging him against me as I kissed him hard enough to remove any doubt. He sighed as his hands slid under my shirt and peeled it away.

His fingers traced a line along my shoulders and he said, "I've had a few wild dreams about you since you went back to the big city."

I ruffled his hair. "Are you trying to say you missed me?"

He grinned as he leaned in to kiss me again. "I *really* wanted you to come back."

It would be a lie to say I hadn't imagined this scene after seeing him last. I'd had regrets. I'd had this dream where I was back in Enza's living room that night, where I played *delicacy* for 72 points and Andre swept the board out of our way and lay his body over mine, covered my mouth with his as he slid his hands along my skin, burning their touch into my memory while the rest of the house was silent with sleep.

"Are you going to tell me about these wild dreams of yours?" I said.

He stood, pulling me to my feet. He held my hand to his mouth, kissed the heel of my hand as he led me down the hallway. "I'd rather show you," he said.

His bedroom was all painted paneling and hard lines, dove gray walls with rustic furniture the color of driftwood. I unbuttoned his shirt and slipped it from his shoulders, dropping it onto a trunk at the foot of the bed. He unfastened my jeans and slid them to the floor, his fingers singeing my skin as they drifted along tender meridians. I unbuckled his belt, and he stepped out of his jeans and boxers, and then we were on the bed, tangled in the sheets, his body pinning mine down as his hands roamed over my breasts, my hips, pinching in the most delightful way.

"Andre," I whispered.

His teeth grazed my earlobe as he said, "I love the way you say that."

My hands gripped his shoulders as I felt his weight shift, felt him hard against my thigh. I tugged at his hair and he sat up abruptly. With his knees on either side of my hips, he stared down at me with a mischievous smile. He fingers slid down my side, across my belly, then lower until I gasped at the pressure in his fingertips. He stayed like that for a few moments, watching me as he teased me, smiling as he made my breath catch in my throat. I closed my eyes, my head back, and the room seemed to fall away, leaving nothing but me, and Andre, and the thrumming of his fingers.

I sighed and he shifted his weight, pulling his hand away.

There was a clatter as he reached behind us into the drawer of the night stand and then he was back, his body holding mine down like it was the only thing that could keep me connected to the earth. He held a packet to his mouth and tore it open with his teeth, and after a moment of fumbling, leaned down and kissed me hard, his teeth pinching my lip, making me shudder. I pulled him closer, called his name again and again until my voice scratched in my throat, until my cries were louder than the thunder that rattled the old windows, until he was all I could feel.

Chapter Six

ANDRE'S ALARM jerked me awake. His arm was draped across my belly, holding me tight against him. There was only a brief moment to enjoy that closeness before he released me from his grip and sat up, pushing the button on his phone to silence it. I turned towards him and he leaned down and kissed me on the shoulder.

"Morning, sunshine," he said.

I grunted a sort of greeting, squinting into the bright sunlight.

"Oh, yeah," he said. "I forgot you're not a morning person." He pulled me against him and kissed me, tickling my sides until I laughed.

"Hey," I said.

"Hey yourself." He stood and went into the bathroom, shutting the door behind him.

I lay there listening to the shower, my mind quickly cluttering with a thousand thoughts. I snapped the rubber band on my wrist to silence them.

When Andre came back out, he was wearing boxers. "What are you doing today?" he asked.

"No plans. Vacation, remember?"

He sat back down on the bed and reached over to push a lock or hair behind my ear. "Spend the day with me," he said.

"Don't you have work?"

He shrugged. "I'll call in a vacation day."

"Aren't you like the only keeper of the peace in the whole parish?"

He grinned, his eyes raking over me, and I wanted to pull him back under the covers.

"I have a deputy," he said, sliding his finger along my neck.

I swatted him with a pillow.

"Let's go out," he said. "Let me show you around."

"Coffee first," I said. "The stronger the better."

He leaned over and kissed me, biting my lip. "That's my girl."

"Also, I should go feed Bella. Swing by the house on our way?"

"Sure," he said. "We should take your car back anyway. I'll go make us a quick breakfast."

He pulled on a pair of jeans and a white pearl-snap shirt that was tight in the shoulders and thin with age. I pulled myself into a sitting position as he went down the hall and into the kitchen. While I dressed, I could hear the notes he hummed hanging in the air like smoke.

At Enza's, there was no sign of Bella. I called for her, shaking the bag of kibble, but she didn't show. I filled her bowl and left it by the door with a saucer of water, hoping she hadn't eaten some dead thing overnight or dug into someone's trash down the road. Andre was a few minutes behind me, making a couple of phone calls to free himself for the day. With the time I had, I took a quick shower and changed into the red printed wrap dress I'd bought with Lucille. When Andre arrived, the dog still hadn't turned up.

"She'll get under the house if it rains," he said. "Let's hit the road."

He wouldn't tell me where we were going, but insisted I wouldn't regret wearing the dress.

We climbed into his pickup truck, an old teal and white Chevrolet with bench seats and a stick shift. With the windows halfway down, my hair was whipping around my cheeks. The sky was gray overhead, the dark trees trembling in the breeze. It seemed Andre was right, that last night's rain had been just the beginning.

When we'd been driving for over half an hour, I said, "At least give me a hint."

"That would ruin the surprise," he said, glancing over ay my bare knees. I'd worn the cowboy boots Lucille had loaned me in case he was planning a walk outside.

I huffed, teasing him, and crossed my arms in mock disgust.

"You said you wanted more surprises, jolie. I'm happy to oblige." He slowed at the next turn and made a hard right onto a gravel road. The force of the turn shoved me towards him and he grinned, sliding his hand over my knee.

The road curved and then we were out of the thick woods and in a clearing with two rows of live oaks with limbs that curled toward the ground, undulating like serpents. Beyond them was a white plantation house, two stories with a four-foot brick foundation, a split staircase that wound from the front doors down either side. It seemed taller than it was wide, a box with black shutters and wide white columns. It had likely stood there for two hundred years. Now, it was restored and open as a museum with a bed and breakfast attached.

The road forked and led us to a small gravel parking lot near the main house. A wooden sign pointed towards the vineyard, the gardens, the lake. A path to the gardens began at the end of the gravel lot and quickly dissolved into the canopy of moss and cypress. The lushness of the green was startling, the blossoms so numerous it was hard to look away. It was like being in an Impressionist painting, bright dabs of color swirling around us.

"I thought we might steal some outdoor time before the storm rolls in," he said.

"This is incredible," I said.

We climbed out of the truck and walked towards the gardens. Andre's hand brushed against mine as we followed the narrow path that wound through the budding trees. Their branches criss-crossed overhead, mingling white blooms with pink buds. Honey bees buzzed all around us, drunk from dipping into endless azaleas. The breeze shifted and brought the tang of brine and earth damp from last night's rain. The air vibrated with the twittering of birds hopping between the branches of shrubs, disguised by veils of leaves.

"What made you want to bring me here?" I said.

"So we could really talk. I can't hear you in the bar." His tone suggested he was only half-joking.

He took my hand and led me over a wooden bridge that arched over a pond filled with lilies. When I rested my elbows on the railing and peered into the water, he leaned next to me, his shoulder touching mine.

"This is one of my favorite places," he said, serious now. "I come here to escape."

"You think I need to escape?"

He smiled, staring out over the water. "We all do sometimes, don't we?"

I wondered how much Lucille had told him.

"I feel like I'm under a microscope in the parish," he said. "I have to be on my best behavior all the time."

"I can see that."

"With everybody watching, I can't do things like this." He leaned over and kissed me, slow and deliberate.

"Scandalous," I said, and he nodded.

"I want to know more about you," he said.

"Like what?"

"Everything," he said.

By late afternoon, we'd wandered through the gardens twice, passing only a few other visitors. Plantations like this one were a big draw for tourists, but we were still in the shoulder season, before school was out and everyone had started traveling for their summer vacations.

Andre led me out of the gardens and across a small meadow by the lake. It had started to rain, just enough to force us indoors. An old barn, probably original, had been painted white and remodeled into a room for wine-tasting with a small restaurant in back. The plantation boasted a small vineyard with its own label, selling a half-dozen varieties of red and white. After tasting each of the wines, we chose a bottle of red to have with dinner.

"I'm really glad you brought me here," I said. "You were right about escape."

He smiled. "You're welcome."

"I think I'm having a mid-life crisis."

He sipped his wine. "Why would you think that?"

"I was doing fine until last year, and then everything fell apart. Work, my engagement, Enza leaving. I was a hot mess when I met you back in December. I thought I had everything figured out. I thought I was headed in the right direction. And it's like the road just crumbled underneath me."

He nodded. "Sometimes that has to happen to get you where you need to be, though."

"You sound like Enza. Don't start telling me the universe is sending signals."

He raised his eyebrows. "We choose our own roads. But that doesn't mean we don't pick bad ones every now and then. Believe me. In my job, I tend to meet people when they've made the worst decisions of their lives."

"Boy, have I made some bad ones."

"We all have," he said, his voice lower. Outside the wind picked up, rattling a shutter against the window. "Maybe you need a change of scenery. A long-term change."

"What, like move down here the way Enza did?"

He shrugged. "Why not?"

"I'd have to sell my house, find a new job—a new career—and start all over again." I sighed, taking a long drink of wine. The thought of starting from scratch again was exhausting, but I'd had the same thought for the last few days. The word *stagnant* had come to mind so often that I felt my life needed evaluation, overhaul. What had been stable and comfortable wasn't making me happy, and I wasn't sure what to change to get myself there. I dropped my hands in my lap and snapped the rubber band. Once. Twice. Three times.

"You might like it down here," he said. "You fit in pretty nicely."

Thunder rolled overhead. "You're a terrible liar."

"Well, it took you a couple days to adjust," he said. "But the bayou suits you." His eyes were wide, greener in the dim light, and for the first time, I was saddened by the idea of leaving on Sunday.

"You know, that's twice you've suggested I move here," I said.

He smiled sheepishly.

The rain drummed louder against the roof. He nodded towards the window behind me as he refilled our wine glasses. "So much for beating the storm home. It must have turned."

The barn shook with another rumble of thunder, the glasses rattling above the bar behind him. Strings of white lights that zig-zagged through the beams above us flickered like a pulse. The barn transformed into the belly of a giant beast that howled and quivered with each gust.

"I've got a crazy idea," he said. His hair was damp from the rain, his lips flushed from the wine. "Let's stay here tonight."

"Get a room here?"

"We'll both escape for a night."

My heart hammered against my ribs as I thought of the night before, the way his fingers tangled in my hair, pulling me close against him. In that moment, it was like I was the only thing that mattered to him. I'd never felt that from anyone before. Now the only fear I had was that I might not feel that way again. The voice of warning in my head had vanished.

"It's probably not safe to drive," I said. "The way the roads wash out and all."

He nodded, a devilish smile appearing.

"Staying here is the sensible thing to do."

His knee brushed against mine. He reached across the table, catching my hand in his. "We have to be sensible," he said, and brought my hand to his lips.

The lights flickered above us, threatening to stay out, and a tingling sensation traveled up my arm like a current.

"Let's get the check," I said.

Our room was all dark wood and green floral wallpaper, a pattern that could have been in the original house. There was a four-poster bed, a dresser with a huge mirror, a vanity with a straight-backed chair, all antiques. Two kerosene lamps were already lit, and some candles were grouped on the dresser and the vanity. Andre struck a match from the box on the dresser and lit the candles as the thunder rumbled outside.

The lights flickered. Andre flipped the switch by the door, leaving us in the glow of candlelight as he closed the space between us. Outside, the lightning flashed blue and rain hammered against the windows. We tumbled onto the bed in a tangle. He sat up, unbuttoning his shirt, and tossed it towards the chair. I laughed, climbing onto his lap as he slipped my dress over my head.

"Good lord, you're a bombshell," he said, and I kissed him until he groaned.

His fingers slid down my back, up and down, as rhythmic as a poem.

When we'd stripped each other bare, he lay me back against the pillows, covering my body with his, pinning me against the cool sheets, exactly where I wanted to be. He slid his stubbled cheek along my neck, kissing some imaginary line between my breasts, along my ribs. I laughed, ticklish, and felt his teeth against my skin as he grinned.

"I love a woman who laughs in bed," he said, his drawl deepened by the wine, and I flinched as thunder split the night sky.

"And I love a man who can make me laugh in bed," I said.

His hands gripped my hips as his mouth moved along the inside of my thigh. I wound my fingers in his hair and pulled his face back up to mine. He smiled a mischievous smile and kissed me hard, making the room spin. I could taste the wine on his lips, smell the salt of the bayou in his hair. He pulled himself away, fumbling for his jeans, and I heard the sound of a foil wrapper tearing. Then his warmth was back, covering my arms, my hips, and his lips were on mine, his breaths ragged in the air between us.

"Andre," I whispered, and he sat up quickly, placing my ankle on his shoulder.

I gasped, and called his name again, and he kissed the top of my foot.

"I'm starting to like these surprises," I said, my voice like gravel.

He grinned, his teeth pinching my foot, and said, "Good. I've still got a few left."

His hands tightened at my waist, his thumbs moving in tiny circles. My back arched and I writhed beneath him, desperate to feel more of him, everywhere. He stared at me, and I couldn't break his gaze, only wanting to be closer still. He teased me with his fingers, his tongue, until at last I cried out and gripped his shoulders, holding him against me.

He breathed my name into my collarbone as his body trembled against mine. When at last he slid over to my side, he dragged one finger from my shoulder to my hip, so slowly it made me ache.

My heart pounded in my ears as the rain slapped against the shingles, and all I could think of was how wrong I'd been to always long for the predictable, and how much I'd miss this man come Monday.

Chapter Seven

I WOKE to bright sunlight and birdsong. My arm was draped over Andre's chest, one leg over his. His arm was tight around my waist, holding me against him. For a moment I lay listening to the slow thumping of his heart, not wanting to break the spell. When I finally looked up at him, he smiled and said, "Hey, you."

"How long have you been awake?" I said, propping myself up on my elbow.

He shrugged. "Half an hour or so."

"You should have just shoved me over to my side if you wanted to get up."

"Why on earth would I do that?" He laced his fingers behind his head.

I sat up, scanning the room for the panties and bra that had been flung from the bed. "Don't you have to get back?"

"It's Saturday," he said. "What's the rush?"

In the night, I'd woken with a start, filled with guilt. I'd dreamed of a hurricane, its winds shattering glass, stripping shingles from the roof, splitting the big oak in Enza's yard right down the middle of its massive trunk. I'd pictured the dog, shivering under broken tree limbs, her teeth gleaming when the lightning crashed around her.

As much as I wanted to stay there with Andre, I knew that I shouldn't.

"I left Bella outside," I said.

It had been raining sideways here, gusts of wind threatening to take down the big pines and magnolias outside our window. It couldn't have been much milder at Enza's house.

"Don't worry," he said. "I'm sure she's fine." He leaned over and kissed me, sliding his hand along my cheek. "This was not her first bad storm," he said. "Let's get some breakfast."

I wanted to believe him, but my gut felt heavy with dread.

We showered and got dressed quickly, then went to the small dining room downstairs. A few other couples had also stayed the night, and we were slow getting our breakfast. I stirred my coffee between sips, hoping I'd find Bella sitting on the porch when we got back. Andre knew I was worried, but kept trying to distract me. I liked that he wanted to put me at ease, but it didn't make me feel any less guilty.

"I could just call Buck and Josie," he said, "and ask them to go check on her."

"Don't bother them," I said, chewing on a biscuit. "You're right. I'm sure she's fine."

"Darlin', she's a swamp dog. She's got webbed feet and a stomach made of steel."

The hostess brought our plates out and I dug in. "I'm sorry," I said. "I'd love to stay out here with you, but I'd just worry about her all day."

He shrugged. "It's fine. Let's go home and check on her, and then we can do something else." He paused, like he was uncertain. "If you want."

"Deal," I said.

"How do you feel about boats?"

My phone buzzed from inside my purse and I fumbled to retrieve it. It was Enza calling, as if she knew I'd done something wrong and could feel the vibration of my worry a hundred miles away.

I frowned at Andre and said, "Hey, Enza. How are you?"

He raised his eyebrows and sipped his coffee.

"Fine," she said. "You getting yourself unwound?"

"Sort of," I said, biting my lip. Had Bella run away to a neighbor's house? Had that neighbor called the number on her tag? Something in Enza's tone made me think she knew something I didn't. "How's your trip?" I asked her.

"Great," she said, "except for that doozie of a storm last night. Any damage at the house?"

"I don't think so," I said.

Andre gave me a quizzical look.

"You haven't been outside yet?" She laughed, and her tone lightened. "I guess the power's on, or you'd be on an emergency coffee run."

"I'm with Andre."

He held his hand up in a wave.

"Ohhhh," she said, teasing. "So dinner turned into a twenty-four hour date, huh?"

I got up from the table and went out onto the porch. When I'd closed the door behind me, I said, "Well, it wasn't planned that way, but here we are."

"You don't have to explain yourself to me. I'm glad you're having fun."

"He is awfully fun." I leaned against the porch railing, my back to the door.

"I had a feeling you two would be good for each other."

"Don't get carried away," I said. "It's just a sleepover."

She groaned. "Stop kidding yourself, Kate."

"What? I'm taking your advice. I'm relaxing. I'm having a good time. No strings."

"I never said no strings." Enza's tone was no longer light. "Any connection that means anything has strings. That's what holds people together."

"I just can't handle anything serious right now. That's all I meant."

She sighed, and there was a long pause that made me think I'd said this all wrong.

"I get it," she said. "You're afraid of being hurt again. That's completely understandable. I'm just saying, don't be so quick to cut him loose."

"He knows this isn't serious. We're just having a fling. He's like my sabbatical boyfriend."

"Kate, I'm not sure he'd think of you this way."

"You're the one who said we'd be good together," I said. "You practically pushed him on me. What's happening here?"

She sighed. "I didn't mean I thought you'd be good for each other for a night, or a weekend," she said. "I meant for real. He's a good man, Kate. The kind you deserve."

"Come on, " I said. "This is like summer camp. He's not serious, either. I'll be gone in a couple days. What else could he think this was?"

A black cat ran past my feet and I jumped. The bell around her neck jingled and her ears flattened. A goldfinch burst from a hedge by the railing and the cat extended one front leg, licking its paw. When I turned back to the door, Andre was staring at me, a sad arch in his eyebrows. He was holding two coffees in to-go cups.

"Hey," I whispered to him. "You ready?"

He walked towards me, then continued down the porch steps without looking at me and said, "I'll wait for you in the truck."

Enza said, "Did you hear me?"

"Sorry," I said, watching Andre stride toward the gravel parking lot. He didn't look back.

"I said we'd like to stay a couple more days, if that's okay with you," Enza said. "Would you want to stay through Wednesday? We could catch up when Jack and I get home."

"Sure," I said, going back into the dining room for my purse. "That's fine."

"Great," she said. "We should be back Tuesday afternoon."

"Okay," I said, but I was only half listening, hurrying across the lawn toward the parking lot where Andre was pacing by the truck.

"Say hi to Andre," she said. "See you soon."

"Yeah, sure," I said, feeling anxious as I approached Andre. "Bye."

I shoved the phone into my bag. Andre leaned against his truck, his hands stuffed into his pockets. The stern look on his face had me worried.

"Hey," I said. "You okay?"

He reached for the coffees sitting on the hood of the truck and handed me one. "Thought you might want one for the road." His tone was bristly.

"Thanks."

He sipped his coffee, but his eyes were colder now, quick to dart past mine. "Did you mean what you told her?" he said. "About this just being a fling?"

I smiled. "You can rest easy. I'm not going to start calling you my boyfriend after two nights together."

"I see." His eyebrows furrowed and his face hardened. There was no smile now. I'd assumed he'd been thinking of us the same way I did, but it was apparent from the set of his jaw that he hadn't. I opened my mouth to say something more kind, but he cut me off.

"What did I ever do to give you the impression you were just a fling?" he said.

For a moment, I said nothing, thinking he might still be teasing me. His silence said that he was not.

"Andre, you've known me for like, a minute, and next week I'll be four states away again."

He crossed his arms. "I've known you since December."

I sighed. "You know what I mean."

"Apparently I need some translation."

"Come on. You weren't wanting me to be something serious. I thought we were on the same page."

"I thought we had something here," he said. "I thought we liked each other."

"Of course I like you. I don't do all the things we've done together with people I don't like. I'm just being practical. I'm a practical person."

"I'm practical, too. And we're good together. Flings aren't practical."

"Long distance isn't practical," I said, getting aggravated.

"Who said anything about long distance?" He flung his arms to his sides, coffee spraying out of the hole in the cup's lid.

"What, you think I'm going to move to the middle of

nowhere? I have a career, a house. What can I do here? There's nothing for me."

He stared at me like I'd slapped him. Then he said calmly, "Then maybe you *should* go home." He opened the door to the truck and climbed inside, the slam of the door shutting me out.

When he started the truck, I strode around to the other side and climbed inside. I braced myself for the squeal of tires, the revving of the engine, wishing there was a chance in hell I could get a cab out here—but Andre Dufresne draped his arm on the back of the bench seat as calmly as if it were a church pew. He peered over the truck's tailgate and eased out of the gravel lot, maneuvering around the other cars as if it was any ordinary day. He turned back to face the windshield and his eyes drifted past me like I wasn't even there.

"Hey," I said, "I didn't mean—"

"You made yourself perfectly clear," he said flatly. "Nothing left to discuss."

And just like that, he was back into matter-of-fact sheriff mode, his heart bulletproof, and I felt as cold as a criminal.

THE DRIVE back to Enza's was the longest ride of my life. When Andre pulled up to the house, my hand hesitated on the door handle for a moment before I climbed out of the truck.

"Do you have all of your things?" he said. It was the first words he'd spoken since we left the plantation.

I nodded, fishing my keys from my purse. "Listen," I said, "I wish you'd talk to me about this. I'm sorry if I—"

"Goodbye, Kate." He turned toward me just long enough for the sunlight to catch bright green flecks in his eyes, and then he was staring over the steering wheel again, waiting for me to leave.

I started to try to explain myself again, but it was evident that he didn't want to hear it. I climbed out and shut the door behind me, and started toward the porch. After I'd let myself in and set my purse down on the kitchen table, I heard the truck rumbling down the driveway.

I'd expected to discover a soggy, furious Bella curled by the front door, but she was nowhere to be found, and her food was uneaten. Even when I walked around the house shaking her bag of kibble, she refused to show herself. The storm had shaken some small limbs from the trees, but there was no real damage. A few shingles had blown off the roof, but that was to be expected down here, where the wind could work itself up into a funnel with no warning. I walked around the yard, calling and whistling for the dog, but she never came.

Mid-afternoon, I called Lucille.

"I messed up," I told her. "I've lost Bella."

"What happened?" she said.

"Well, technically I didn't lose her, but she's missing. Since yesterday. Maybe the day before."

When I told her about going to Andre's, and getting home late, and then being gone during the storm, she sighed and said, "Did you call Enza?"

"I was hoping I wouldn't have to. Has she ever gone missing like this? Could she be at a neighbor's or something?"

"Jack's never mentioned it to me. I'd come help you, but I'm still in Baton Rouge. I was headed back tomorrow."

I groaned, pacing in the backyard. "Is there a shelter around here?"

"There's one a half hour away," she said. "Doubt anyone

would take her that far, though. People don't really do that around here. Besides, everyone knows Bella."

"I messed up with Andre, too."

She made an exasperated sound. "You just said you spent the night at an inn."

"Yeah, and then we had a disagreement. Kind of a big one."

"Oh," she said.

"I said something without thinking. Something that hurt him."

She sighed. "It happens. Part of the human condition, unfortunately."

I sat down on the ground, feeling weak. This town was turning me inside out. My instincts were wrong about everything. "I feel like an ass," I told her.

After a pause she said, "If you want to fix it, you should talk to him."

"He's got zero interest in talking to me."

"Let him cool off for a day," she said. "Underneath all that brass, he's kind of a softie."

The woods were already dark beyond the lake, but I walked along the tree line, calling for Bella. I heard a rustling in the brush and went to investigate, thinking maybe her collar had gotten snagged in a limb. The leaves shook on the shrub as I approached, calling her name again and again. I was furious that I'd left her and that I'd hurt Andre. I had to fix this damage I'd done.

The bush quivered as a hen-sized bird burst from the branches. My heart thudded against my breastbone and I gasped, jumping backwards. The bird shrieked and flapped its wings as it flew into the tree above. I tripped on a root and toppled onto the ground, hitting hard on my hip.

"Dammit," I hissed, my hip stinging. I got up and dusted myself off, calling again for the dog as I peered into the darkness. It was impossible to see anything, the sun setting and the woods in shadow. I considered walking through the swamp with a flashlight, but I'd seen those horror movies, and I knew how they ended. If an alligator didn't maul me, at the very least I would twist my ankle and chip a tooth as I crashed to the ground and smashed my face against a rock. I was not a gal who belonged in the woods at night. That was undeniable.

After leaving the food and water on the porch again, I went inside to make my own dinner. Enza hadn't left me much in the way of groceries, but she'd left the makings for spaghetti. I diced a green pepper and an onion and tossed them into a skillet with some beef, and thought about Andre. I felt bad about saying what I'd said that morning. But our coming together had just seemed like a natural progression: we were both a little lonely, and we were having fun together. I needed a little affection, and thought he did, too. The practical part of me said he wouldn't expect our being together to be more—it didn't make sense for this to be more than a fling. I figured he was practical enough to feel the same way.

One thing was certain. I wasn't used to reading things so wrong.

I dumped a big can of tomato sauce into the skillet and turned it down to simmer. Over-thinking things had made a mess of my romantic life, but it seemed that I'd not given Andre enough thought. I pulled my cell phone from my pocket and checked for missed calls or texts.

There were none.

I considered texting him, but what on earth would I say? Sorry I slept with you? Sorry I made this complicated? Sorry I don't know how to function in a grown-up relationship?

The hours rolled by as I lay reading on the couch and snapping that stupid rubber band every time I thought about Andre. At last, I pulled it off my wrist and shot it across the living room. Out on the porch there was a thumping sound against the floorboards, the rattle of the metal dish of kibble. I went to the door and felt a wave of relief when I saw a furry brown body in the darkness. That relief quickly turned to disgust when I opened the door and turned on the porch light.

A raccoon sat on its haunches, shoving bits of dog food into its mouth with front paws that looked eerily like tiny human hands. My cursing startled the coon, and it scrambled off the porch and into the night. I walked into the yard, calling one last time for Bella. My voice came out hoarse, desperate. A pair of yellow eyes gleamed at the edge of the woods, but didn't move towards me as I called. When the eyes blinked into darkness, I went back inside.

Sometimes I wished it was possible to smash all these awkward, misshapen, imperfect actions of my life and use their dust to make decisions that were better.

I couldn't even do a one-night stand right. And I'd lost the damned dog.

Chapter Eight

THE NEXT MORNING, there was still no sign of Bella. My coffee tasted bitter. The harsh morning light felt like it sliced through me when I walked outside. I called the dog, my voice ragged, and ventured into the woods where the ground turned soggy and soft beneath my feet. The wind whistled through the trees, rattling their leaves and twice I stopped cold, certain I'd heard barking. When the breeze settled down, there was only the chirping of birds, the chatter of squirrels. After an hour, I went back into the house to find Enza's keys.

Determined not to be outdone, I drove along the back roads near Enza's house, leaving the top off the Jeep. The main highway carried me all the way into the town of Bayou Sabine, which was really just one main street with a few stop lights. I walked around for a while, hoping I might find Bella crouched behind a restaurant, or napping under the shade of a bench by the ice cream shop, but I was three miles from Enza's house. Would the dog wander this far? I asked a few shop owners if they'd seen a dog on the loose, but none had seen a gray bob-tail like Bella. I checked the bulletin boards in the post office, just in case someone had pinned up a flyer for a found dog, but there was only a photo of a black lab.

No Bella.

Defeated, I climbed back into the Jeep and doubled back toward the house on a different road that went alongside a canal, heading deeper into the swampland. There was thick brush along the road most of the way, with deep cypress groves that were dark even in daylight. I drove slowly, calling for Bella every now and then, imagining her popping out of the brush at any moment, tail wagging and tongue lolling.

But she never appeared.

Back at the house, I sank onto the steps of the porch, feeling like the wind had been knocked out of me. I felt like a terrible friend. I didn't know how to fix this. Why couldn't I have just come home early that first night with Andre? The thought of calling Enza to ask for help made me sick to my stomach. She would hate me for this. Jack would hate me. I tried not to imagine the dog dead in the swamp or in a ditch, hit by a car. I closed my eyes, pressed the heels of my hands against my cheeks, blocking out the sun. I pictured Bella wandering up into the yard, emerging from the swamp behind the house like a ghost. I willed her to come home, hoping my thoughts might lead her back. Dogs were smart. Couldn't they pick up on our brain waves? Shouldn't she know how badly I needed her to return? *Come back*, I thought, pushing the command out onto the breeze. *Come home.*

Over and over, I said the words, and I realized that it wasn't just Bella I pictured emerging from the woods. I wanted Andre to come back to me, too. I wanted him to walk up from the cypress grove, to stride towards me in that slow, confident way of his, to take my hand and walk by my side toward the next surprise. So many parts of my life were uncertain now, but there was one thing I was sure about: I did not want what was happening with Andre to be over. I didn't want to be without him, and though I didn't understand exactly what that meant yet, I needed to find out.

I'd felt something with him that I hadn't in a long, long time: delight. The real kind that lights you up from within. The kind that makes you forget about everything else.

I'd thought of him as a fling because flings couldn't hurt me. We keep those people at a distance: close enough to enjoy, but far enough away so they can't crack through our walls and find our weak spots. That's what I'd told myself, anyway.

Behind me, the bottles that hung in the oak clinked and howled in the breeze. When at last I opened my eyes, I was certain that Bella would be trotting towards me through the grass.

But there was only a dove, pecking in the sand.

THERE WAS ONLY one other thing to do. I fished my cell phone from my satchel and dialed Andre's cell. When he didn't answer, I called the number on the card he gave me.

"Sheriff's department," he said.

I started, expecting someone besides the sheriff himself to answer. "Andre," I said. "It's Kate."

There was a pause. "Hello," he said, his voice cool.

My throat felt like it would swell shut. "I need help. I don't know who else to call."

His voice softened as he went into protector mode. "What's happened? Are you all right?"

I sighed, relieved to hear the sternness in his voice diminish. "I'm fine. But I lost Bella. She's been gone since the other night, when the storm first hit."

Another pause.

"I went all over looking for her," I said. "I put food out, I searched all through the woods, I called the shelter. I just don't know what else to do. I have to find her, Andre. Could you help me? Please?" My breath caught on the last word, and for the first time I felt like I might cry.

"The last time you saw her was before you came to my house?" he said. "That's almost three days."

I felt sick. "Has she ever done this with Jack? Run away?"

"Not for this long," he said. There was a heavy sigh, some rustling of papers in the background. "Let me see if I can knock off early today and help you look."

"Thank you," I said. "I'll owe you big time." I cringed as soon as the words were out. "I mean, I'd really appreciate it. I'm at a loss, and Enza will kill me."

"You didn't call her?" he said.

"I'm hoping we find her so I never have to have this conversation with Enza. Or Jack. They'll never trust me again."

"Hmm," he said, letting out a long breath. And I could read between his words. I knew he was thinking that he couldn't trust me either, that I deserved this for treating him the way I did—and hell, maybe he was right. Maybe this was a karmic lesson, but I really needed karma to step back and teach me using something of my own, and not my best friend's dog.

"I'll swing by your house in a little while," he said.

"Thank you," I said, but he hung up before I got the words out.

It was after four o'clock when Andre came down the lane in his marked Jeep Cherokee. I rushed outside and hopped inside the passenger side. "Thanks for coming," I said. "Really."

His jaw was set in a hard line, his eyes hidden behind amber aviator glasses. "I do more missing persons cases than missing dogs," he said, turning toward me just slightly. "Let's keep this one between you and me, since we're on the taxpayers' time."

"I feel terrible about this. It's all my fault." I gave him a lingering look, swallowed hard after the words.

He pulled out of the drive and headed toward the highway. "Maybe not entirely." He glanced over at me, one eyebrow arched.

"I was thoughtless."

"Dogs run away. It's not unusual."

"I was being selfish, wanting to stay with you," I said. "I shouldn't have left her outside for so long,"

"I wouldn't have risked driving you in that storm. It wasn't safe." There was a note of tenderness in his voice. He turned off the highway, where there were ruts in the grass, but not packed dirt.

"Is this even a road?" I said.

"Fire road," he said. "It winds back around alongside the canal. I figure it's more likely she's out in the woods somewhere. If someone found her, they'd have called Jack."

My stomach lurched. Paranoid, I pulled my phone from my

pocket and checked for any missed calls or texts from Enza. Surely she would have contacted me if someone had called Jack and said they had his dog, right? She wouldn't keep that from me.

There were no missed calls from Enza. No texts.

We lumbered through the woods, tree branches scraping the sides of the vehicle, the weeds hissing as they were flattened beneath the undercarriage. A gray blur caught my eye and I leaned out the window, but it was only a bundle of Spanish moss tangled in the briars. Egrets dotted the trees above us, preening in the afternoon sun. A chorus of frogs chirped a call-and-response from the thickets, their voices throbbing like a pulse.

The road followed the canal for what seemed like miles. Andre kept one hand on the wheel, one hand in his lap, the windows down. Every few hundred yards, he'd stop and whistle the way Jack did, two fingers in his mouth, splitting the air and startling the birds. The road emptied us back onto the highway and Andre drove slowly, pulling onto the shoulder when cars came up behind him.

When I couldn't take his stonewalling anymore, I said, "I feel like I should explain something to you. About what happened the other day."

"You explained yourself pretty well," he said. "After." He pulled over abruptly to let a car pass, jostling me against the window.

"Okay, I probably deserve that."

He pulled back onto the road, glancing in the rearview.

"I'm just not good at this, Andre. I'm good in the moment, but not for the long haul."

His jaw softened, just slightly.

"I never meant to hurt your feelings. It was stupid, what I said to Enza."

"Let's just focus on finding the dog," he said, slinging us around a curve.

I sighed, scanning the shoulder of the road. "Plus, it was a lie."

He turned towards me, a puzzled expression on his face. We came out of the curve and I shrieked. An animal was just ahead, by the side of the road, a heap of gray-brown fur. A buzzard hovered over it, flapping its great black wings as we approached. My heart felt like it was squeezed by a fist.

"Oh god. Pull over," I said, pointing. Andre stepped on the brake, and I was already yanking on the door handle. I sank into the soft grass along the shoulder as I ran, hoping I was wrong, that it was a coyote, a fox, anything but a dog.

But it was a dog.

The buzzard fixed its fishlike eye on me and hopped a few feet away as Andre jogged to catch up. I stopped a few inches from the animal and stared at its mangled limbs.

Andre put his hand on my shoulder and said, "It's not her."

I doubled over, a wave of relief and disgust hitting me like a punch.

Andre pointed. "Look. Big fluffy tail. Not Bella."

I wanted to curl up against him, but he took his hand off my shoulder and said, "Come on. Let's keep looking. We're losing daylight."

"We can't just leave it here," I said. "Pecked at by buzzards, hit by another car. Would you want your kid to find his pet this way?"

"It won't be here long. Some gator'll come drag it off." He said this with zero emotion, as if he were telling me whether he preferred sugar or cream in his coffee. It stung to hear his voice so callous. Because of me.

"Even more reason to not leave it," I said. "Then the owners would never know what happened to it."

"Are you suggesting we bury it? Right here by the road?"

"Don't you have a shovel in that giant vehicle?"

He sighed, planting his hands on his duty belt. "If we bury it, they'll still never know."

"So we call the number on the tag and tell them."

He raked a hand through his hair, then walked back towards the Cherokee. He rummaged around in the back for a minute, then came back to me carrying a blue tarp under his arm. He unfolded it partway on the ground and pulled a pair of disposable gloves from his pocket. He snapped a glove on to each hand, then knelt down over the dog and removed its collar.

He looked at the silver heart-shaped tag and said, "I'll call the owner to let them know the animal was found on the highway. I can take care of it if they don't ask to see it." He put the collar in a plastic bag and slipped it into his pocket, then gently lifted the dog and placed it on the tarp. He folded the plastic over and carried it back to the Cherokee, then placed it the back of the vehicle with the jumper cables and fire extinguisher.

I followed him back to the car and got inside. The buzzard hopped back over to the spot where the dog had been, leaning close to the earth, turning its cold eye back to us.

Inside the car, Andre took the bag with the collar from his pocket and dropped it into the cup holder in the console between us.

"It's better this way," I said. "No one wants to live with not knowing."

He started the car, staring straight ahead as he drove. After a while, he turned back onto the road to Enza's house. The sun was already starting to dip below the tallest trees.

"What are you doing?" I said.

"It's getting late," he said. "There's nothing we can do after dark. And I've got to do something about the dog in the back. Can't leave it there for the morning deputy."

My eyes stung with tears. It wasn't supposed to be like this. The Cherokee rumbled down the dirt lane to the house. I wanted to tell him how wrong I'd been, how I'd been lying to myself, how I hated the thought of never seeing him again and leaving him hurt this way. But my head ached, and my heart felt like it was being crushed in a vise, and I just wanted to slide beneath the surface of the lagoon, the way so many creatures did out here.

He left the engine running as he said, "I'm sorry we couldn't find her."

"I'm sorry, too," I said, my voice nearly a whisper. I climbed out of the car and shut the door. I didn't know how to say the rest.

I walked toward the house, fumbling to dig the key out of my jeans pocket. As I unlocked the door, I turned back toward the road. Andre was still in the driveway, the engine idling. I stepped inside and stood for a moment, the door nearly closed, wishing he'd turn off the engine and come inside the house. After a few breaths, I flung the door open, all set to charge into the yard and sit on the hood of his car if that's what it took to get him to talk to me.

But he was already headed back toward the highway, a cloud of dust hanging in the air between us.

LATER, when the moon was high and I was halfway through a bottle of red wine, I almost called Enza and confessed everything. I'd pulled up her number and had chickened out twice. While my finger hovered over the screen, I heard a thumping sound outside the door. At first, I thought of Andre, and for one moment was hopeful that it was his boots on the porch, that he'd come back to talk to me—but then I heard the rattle of the screen door. I ran into the hallway and flipped on the porch light. When I opened the door, there was Bella, pawing at the screen.

She was filthy, covered in mud from nose to tail, pieces of grass stuck in her fur. When I opened the door, she ran inside and pranced in a circle around me, leaving bits of mud all around us.

"Bella," I said, and kneeled down to pet her. She licked at my hands, still hopping from foot to foot. Her collar was gone and her ear had a small cut. I checked her over, looking for any other wounds, but couldn't see anything but dirt.

"Come with me," I said, and she trotted by my heels as I led her into the downstairs bathroom. I'd forego the inflatable pool tonight and wash her in the bath tub. There was no way I was going to risk her taking off into the woods again.

After she was washed and fluffed—and fed—she jumped onto the sofa with me and lay her head on my thigh. "How about a movie?" I said, flipping the television on. She let out a heavy sigh and I ruffled her fur. I texted Lucille and told her she'd come home, that everything was fine.

But that was only half true.

I started to call Andre, but hated the idea of hearing his

voice so cool and gravelly, as if I were as disappointing as the hooligans he locked up on the weekends. Finally, I sent him a text.

Bella came home, I wrote.

After a few minutes, he texted back: *Good.*

She must have gotten tangled in the swamp, I wrote. *Her collar's gone and she's scratched up.*

Does she need a vet? he wrote.

No, she's ok. It felt good to talk to him, even if it was in clipped text messages. It made me think for a brief moment that there might be hope for us, if I could just get him talking to me again, if he would just let me explain. I'd tell him how much this week had meant to me, how I wanted to figure out a way to keep seeing him because he seemed like the best thing that had happened to me in a very long time.

I waited for another response from him. When the screen remained dark, I wrote *I really am sorry.* What I wanted to say was *I was kidding myself, I was falling for you, I've never been so sickened by the thought of not seeing someone again. I was scared.*

But what I said instead was: *I was an idiot.*

After thirty minutes, there was still no reply.

Copy that, I thought.

Chapter Nine

MONDAYS HAVE ALWAYS BEEN loathsome for me. This one began around three in the morning, when Bella woke me by licking the heel of my foot. I'd sat straight up in the bed, dreaming I was moments from being devoured by an alligator, so tangled in the sheets I'd nearly tumbled onto the floor. When Bella curled up next to me, I lay awake ruffling her fur, listening to her snore, and suddenly realized that I had never changed my return flight after talking to Enza on Saturday. I was supposed to have been on a plane twelve hours before and somehow had completely forgotten that fact.

I did not miss flights.

I did not have flings.

I did not walk away from people who mattered.

The ticket was gone, the money wasted. I'd have to just buy a one-way ticket now, or rent a car to drive home. I'd been so preoccupied with Andre, with the lost Bella, that I'd stopped trying to solve my biggest problem. The whole point of taking this time off was to decide what to do now that my job at the lab was over, and I'd pushed it so far into the back of my mind that I had neglected it completely. I was no closer to a solution than I was when I left. I had no plan.

It was not like me to avoid problems. What was happening to me down here?

The problem I really wanted to solve, though, was Andre.

I'd done exactly what I'd been afraid of: I'd wrecked whatever was building between us, like Godzilla knocking over a skyscraper with one scaly flailing arm. The worst part was that I'd lied when I told Enza that Andre was just a fling. It had been easy to think of him that way, because that kept him at a safe distance, where he couldn't hurt me. But I'd been so preoccupied with keeping myself from getting too close to him, saving myself from being hurt, that I'd put him in a place where I could hurt him.

The truth was, I didn't want to walk away and never see him again. I didn't know how to make this work between us, but I wanted to figure out a way. Andre was pushing me away because he was hurt. He didn't want to see me, but I had to change that.

After coffee, I browsed the flights online and bought a one-way ticket back to Raleigh-Durham. Then I called the sheriff's office.

A woman answered this time, her voice far too chipper for a Monday.

"Is Sheriff Dufresne in today?" I asked her.

"Yes, but he's in a lunch meeting," she said. "Can I take a message or put you through to the deputy?"

"No, thank you," I said. "I'll call back later."

Later, I shoved the bottle of wine from the plantation into my purse and got Bella into the car. She narrowed her eyes at me when I strapped her into the passenger side with the seat belt, but she relented with one final snort. Driving felt like leaving, and I didn't like that feeling. I stopped at the grocery store and then went to Andre's house. His truck wasn't in the driveway. It was just after three o'clock, so he was most likely still at work. I knocked on the door anyway, just to be sure.

When there was no answer, I searched the porch for a spare key. I tried under the mat, under the flower pots at the corner of the porch, and under what looked like a fake rock by the hedges. Then I went around to the back porch and ran my fingers along the top of the doorframe.

Bingo. No one ever checks up high.

I let myself in through the screened-in back porch, and walked through the house calling Andre's name, just in case. When he'd sneaked in on me that day, I'd clocked him with a hair dryer. The stakes were a little higher when you snuck into the sheriff's house.

Finding no sign of him, I went back to the car and freed Bella, letting her romp around for a while before confining her to the screened-in porch. I retrieved the groceries from the car and started in on dinner—a meal that I hoped would at least convince the sheriff to talk to me.

I'D PUT the lasagna in the oven at five o'clock, but it was nearly seven by the time I heard Andre's truck rumble down the driveway. I'd made myself at home, watching an old sea-serpent movie on TV and helping myself to a generous shot of the bourbon I'd left here the last time we had dinner together. A gal had to fortify herself for dinners like this one.

Bella barked from her spot on the back porch and I heard Andre muttering as he walked up onto the front steps. He opened the door without even trying his key in the lock and paused in the hallway as I came out of the living room.

"Hello," he called.

"It's me," I said, coming into the hall. "Don't shoot."

He frowned, his hands on his hips. "What are you doing here? Practicing breaking and entering?" His voice was cool.

"I cooked you dinner," I blurted. This encounter had seemed more romantic in my head. I was determined not to say all the wrong things this time.

"Why would you do that?" He walked past me into the kitchen and glanced at the table, set for two.

"It's phase one of my proper apology."

"Is that lasagna?"

I nodded. "There's also chocolate pecan pie."

He cocked one eyebrow, as if weighing hunger against anger.

"It stays whether I do or not," I said, "but I was hoping you'd let me stay, too. At least through the main course."

He unbuttoned the top button of his uniform shirt and sighed. "Let me go get changed."

"This can't wait." I placed my hands on his biceps and steered him towards the chair. "Sit. Please." I knew I had to tell him soon, before my thoughts started to spin, dissolving my courage.

He opened his mouth as if to protest, but he sat.

I paced in front of him, trying to find the right words. This was important. I had to get it right this time.

"Kate," he started, scratching his stubbled chin.

"This makes me feel nervous, you in that uniform. I feel like a criminal."

"I was going to change my clothes," he said. "You stopped me."

"Never mind."

I sat next to him at the table and poured two glasses of wine, then quickly took a sip.

Andre eyed me warily and turned the bottle to read the label. "This is from the plantation," he said.

"I bought one before we left. I wouldn't want to drink it with anyone else."

He ran a hand through his hair and said, "Look, Kate, I get it."

"I don't think you do." I moved my chair closer to him. "I didn't get to finish telling you something the other day. When we were out looking for Bella."

"Okay," he said. His eyes had darkened in the dim light.

"What I said to Enza that day was a lie. I don't know why I told her you were a fling. That's not the way I felt about you."

He took a long sip of wine, then leaned his elbows on the table. His eyes looked tired, like he hadn't been sleeping well.

I placed my hand on his knee. "The truth is, I felt that way in the beginning, like maybe you wanted something casual, too. And then it started to feel different, and that scared me. I didn't want to admit the way I felt about you, because I thought it just meant I'd get hurt again. And I didn't want that to happen. Not with you."

He stared at me for a moment. "How did you feel, Kate?"

I chewed my lip, then took a long drink from my own glass. His eyes were fixed on me, as if trying to read beneath the surface. I didn't know the best way to say this, how to make him understand. This was my last chance. His furrowed brow said he was skeptical, one moment closer to giving up on me.

"Things just feel right with you. I don't feel like I have to plan everything and figure out all the details. I've felt more alive this week than I have in a long time, and that's because of you."

He stared at me, as if he didn't quite believe me.

"Hang on," I said. I grabbed my purse from the empty chair and rummaged through it until I found the boarding pass I'd printed.

I handed him the pass and said, "Flings end, and people go their separate ways. But I don't want that. I don't want to not see you again."

He looked at the boarding pass and said, "This flight is next Tuesday."

I nodded. "You said once that we had something. I think we have something, too." I put my hand back on his knee and said, "I was so glad you walked into that bar when I was out with Lucille. I was so happy you asked me to dinner. Every day I wanted to see you more the next day."

"I thought you wanted to go home. To your job, to your house."

I shook my head. "I hate my job. I need something different, and I like being with you. I don't want this to be over just because I said something stupid."

"You said there was nothing for you here."

"I was angry. Don't you ever say stupid things when you're mad?"

He sighed. "I say all the stupid things."

I squeezed his knee. "If I leave now, I'll regret it. Maybe the rest of my life."

He stared at me, a storm in his eyes. "Your lab—they gave you another week off?"

I laughed. "I sent my boss an email saying I'd be gone another week. If they don't like that, they can fire me. I don't care."

"You've been body-snatched," he said.

"I know when I've found something worth pursuing."

Andre sipped his wine, his eyes fixed on me.

"You make me more spontaneous. I like that. I need that."

His face was unreadable. "I don't know what to say."

"Say you'll let me try again," I said, "and I won't be a jerk this time."

His lip curved in a tiny smile. "We're all jerks sometimes."

"Is that a yes?" I said.

He stood up from the table, and my heart thumped so hard it hurt.

"I think you're worth pursuing, too," he said. He reached for my hand and pulled me to my feet, and then his hands were cupping my cheeks and he was kissing me, tenderly at first, and then so deeply I could barely breathe. I tangled my fingers in his hair and he lifted me, set me down on the counter. When he leaned back for a moment, I wrapped my legs around his waist.

"Aren't you starving?" I said, nodding towards the table.

"Dying," he said, sliding his stubbled cheek along my neck. "Dinner can wait."

I laughed as he tickled me, fumbling with the buttons of his shirt. He leaned his forehead against mine and said, "I hated the idea of you leaving. Of never seeing you again."

"Me, too."

"I wonder what we can do with all that time," he said, his lips brushing my ear. "Tuesday's a long ways away." His hands held me firmly against him, and my mind didn't even drift to next Tuesday, or what might come after in all the days that followed. I was content to be firmly planted in that one moment, dizzy with delight.

There was no other place I wanted to be.

Want more of the Bayou Sabine series?

How did Kate and Enza end up in little Bayou Sabine, anyway? See how the series begins as Enza goes to Louisiana to uncover family secrets and gets more trouble than she bargained for in BAYOU MY LOVE.

Somewhere near Bayou Sabine, Louisiana

I'D SPENT THE NIGHT somewhere in east Mississippi, in a motel that served moon pies and instant coffee as continental breakfast. It was a blessing I was exhausted when I checked in—I didn't notice much about the place and was able to sleep the peaceful slumber of a person ignorant of potential health hazards. Ordinarily, I wouldn't stay in a place like the Teddy Bear Motel, but around midnight, I'd finally gotten too tired to keep driving. It was the only place around. So I'd stripped the comforter off the bed, skipped the shower and brushed my teeth quickly, not staring too hard at the sink or counter. Too much scrutiny of that place and I'd itch all the way to Bayou Sabine.

A little after noon, it was already scorching. I cursed myself for not getting the Jeep's air conditioning fixed back in the spring. With the windows down, I tried to convince myself the heat wasn't so bad, but my clothes were sticking to me. The land around me had shifted from rolling hills to marshland, and at last I felt like I was out of my father's orbit. I was thinking less of him and more about those summers I'd spent at the big blue house on the bayou, Vergie teaching me to play poker while we sat on the porch. Starting in grade school, I'd visit her for nearly three months every June when school let out. It was my favorite time of the year. I could run around barefoot and go swimming in the creek at night, and I didn't have to be ladylike—ever. With Vergie, life seemed more magical. Anything was possible when I was with her.

As I opened the last moon pie I'd smuggled from the motel, I was hit with a flash from years before.

Vergie and I were sitting on a quilt in one of the old cemeteries, back in a corner under an oak tree with limbs that undulated along the ground like tentacles. She was telling me ghost stories while we had tea and beignets, the powdered sugar clinging to our noses. We sat still as tombstones while a funeral procession passed, the people dancing as music filled the whole sky.

"Why are those people having such a good time?" I asked. "Isn't that a funeral?"

"That's the grandest way you can say goodbye to someone," Vergie said.

Vergie's own funeral had been tame compared to the scene that day, and now I felt bad that we hadn't given her a send-off like that one. She would have appreciated that, and I would have remembered if I hadn't stayed away so long.

Why had it taken me fifteen years to come back?

I turned my thoughts back to the house as I crossed the state line. Six weeks wasn't much time.

I pulled off the interstate onto a smaller highway. From there on, the roads would get narrower until they carried me into the little community of Bayou Sabine. I vaguely remembered the way, but with all the canals out here, the roads start to look the same. It's beautiful—don't get me wrong—but if you were to turn me around three times and plop me down in the middle of this marshland, I'd likely never see North Carolina again.

I checked the GPS on my phone, but the road wasn't showing up.

"Oh, come on," I said, swiping my thumb across the screen. The red dot that was supposed to be me was now off the nearest named road. According to the GPS, I was in a bayou. I glanced up at the road, trying to get my bearings and not swerve into the water for real.

Signal lost, it said. I groaned, restarting the app. When I looked up, an alligator was lumbering across the road—all six feet of him stretched across my lane.

"Oh, hell!" I slammed the brake to the floor, flinching as the tires squealed and the Jeep fish-tailed. I bit my lip so hard I tasted blood, and I called that gator everything but a child of God. I expected to hear a terrible thud at any second. Swerving, I missed him by just a few inches, but I was close enough to see his catlike eye as I shot across the opposite lane and onto the shoulder. Off to my left, there was nothing but swamp and black mud. I gripped the wheel, fighting to stay on the hard ground.

The Jeep stopped on what felt like solid earth, the weeds as high as the door handle. My heart hammered in my chest. Vergie used to tell me old voodoo legends about alligators, how they were tricksters, always causing trouble.

Please don't be stuck. Not out here.

My foot eased the gas pedal down, and the Jeep inched forward. The tires spun as I pushed harder. "This is not happening."

A rusty pickup rumbled toward me. The driver gave me a long look, but he hardly slowed down. I nudged the Jeep into four wheel drive and turned the tires as I hit the gas. It rocked a few times, then lurched forward and caught hold of the grass before crossing onto the pavement. I glanced back to where the alligator had crossed, but it was gone.

"Welcome back," I muttered to myself.

The old two-lane highway cut the land in half, with swamps on one side and pastures on the other. With the black water so close, I felt like the earth might open up and devour me at will. The trees were full of moss, the water creeping up their trunks like it was swallowing them.

I passed Vergie's driveway the first time, not recognizing it until I caught a glimpse of the pale blue goose she'd left by the mailbox like a sentinel. The paint was peeling, but the goose stood firmly in a patch of daylilies, just as it had since I was a girl. I turned around and eased onto the dirt drive. I felt the hollow in my chest expand, the void Vergie had left.

Cypress trees lined the road to the house, their limbs curling toward the ground. The breeze tickled the drooping leaves of the trees, and in the distance I heard the faint clink of glass, like a wind chime. Just beyond the house stood a spirit tree, bottles hanging from its branches like Christmas ornaments. It had been there long before Vergie, but she had added a few herself after drinking pints of bourbon and gin. She used to tell me those bottles captured evil spirits, kept them from roaming through the bayou and attaching themselves to good folks that lived nearby. I'd never really believed they held ghosts, but I liked the sound of the wind whistling over the lips of the bottles. Now, as the light glinted blue and green in the leaves of the tree, the sound felt more melancholy than soothing.

This place had a wildness that was hard not to like. It smelled sweet like magnolia, bitter like the swamp. Egrets dotted the trees like blooms of cotton, preening themselves in the slivers of sunlight. The driveway wound back into the woods, hidden from the main road. Patches of gravel mixed with the soil, packed hard from the heat and drought. When at last I pulled into the yard, I was surprised at how small the house seemed compared to my memory of it. It was still plenty big at two stories high, but it was a paler shade of blue than I remembered, and the roof was missing some shingles. The porch was cluttered with potted flowers, strings of lights hanging from the eaves, and a hammock strung between two corner posts. I could almost see Vergie's silhouette in the rocker, and I knew then that I was going to prove my father wrong.

I had to. I owed it to Vergie. This place was a part of her, and it was a part of me now too. I had to do this right.

It wasn't until I saw a pair of feet dangling from the hammock that I noticed the truck parked under a tree at the edge of the yard. A small dark pickup with patches of rust like spots on a horse. I squinted at the feet, thinking surely I was seeing something that wasn't there. But there was no mistaking the shape in the hammock, the lazy swinging motion.

I leapt from the car and slammed the door so hard that a head rose above the banister. My father had dealt with squatters once or twice, but I hadn't thought they'd move in so fast. Striding toward the steps, I cursed myself for not coming by when I was in town for the funeral.

I tried to cool my temper and concentrated on the sound of my boot heels pounding the dirt. There was no turning back now, because the man had definitely seen me.

He sat up in the hammock, and I swallowed hard as I reached the steps.

The man's hair was rumpled, as if he'd slept in that hammock all night. His shirt, rolled at the wrists, was pushed up just enough from his pants that I could see a thin band of tan skin above his belt. He appeared to be only a few years older than me, but had tiny wrinkles around his eyes and lips that suggested he'd spent more time in the sun. And he looked familiar. My mind raced, trying to figure out where I'd seen him before.

"Hi there," he said, sitting up straight. "Are you lost?"

"No," I said, planting my hands on my hips. *Be calm*, I thought. *This doesn't have to get ugly.*

"I don't get too many visitors. I figured you took a wrong turn off the main road. You'd have to be lost to end up out here." His drawl made my ears tingle in a nice way, but the way he lounged in the hammock like he owned the place made me want to push him out of it head first.

"How about you tell me who you are," I said. "And what you're doing here."

He sat up straighter, running his hands through his dark

hair. It was short, but stood out in tufts, as if the wind had pulled it through the holes in the hammock. "I believe it's customary for the interloper to identify herself to the current inhabitant," he said, half-smiling. "Not the other way around."

"This is my house," I said, trying to hold my temper down. "So that makes you the interloper."

He chuckled. "Darlin', I think you've got me confused with somebody else that lives in the middle of nowhere. Who are you looking for?" His tone was even, as if this kind of encounter happened every week.

"I'm not looking for a who," I said. "I'm looking for a house. This house. And last I checked, I didn't have any long-lost cousins living in it."

He glanced around him. "Well, one of us is in the wrong place. And it ain't me." His dark blue eyes held me in a warm gaze that in any other situation would make me want to lean in closer.

"This is my grandmother's house," I said, no longer caring when or where I might have seen him before. The priority was my property.

He cocked his head. "You mean Vergie?" His eyes lit up. "Well, why didn't you say so, darlin'?" He eased out of the hammock as slow as a river. Even his voice swaggered, and I imagined what it would sound like against my ear.

I shook my head to erase the thought.

When he stood, he smoothed his shirt down against his body. Tall and muscular, he towered over me, and I'm no small woman. His shirt was snug against his broad shoulders, pulled taut across his biceps. He held out his hand, smiling like I was some long lost friend, and in spite of myself, I shook it.

"I'm Jack Mayronne," he said. His big hand squeezed mine,

and I swallowed hard as something that felt like static electricity rippled down my arm.

"Enza Parker," I said, struggling to keep my voice firm. "You knew my grandmother?" The nagging feeling returned. Where had I seen him? At this house when I was a teenager? Recently, when I was back for the funeral? I'd blocked so many of those images from my mind, and right now was not the time to try to recover them.

His thumb slid along my palm, and I saw a tattoo peeking out from under the sleeve of his shirt, a black curve like a snake. I wondered how far up it went.

"Sure," he said, holding my hand a little too long. "She was a fine lady. And if you come from that stock, I guess you're all right."

"That still doesn't explain what you're doing in her house."

He grinned, shoving his hands into his pockets. He looked like he could have come from a rodeo, in his faded jeans and plaid pearl-snap shirt. "You're just as feisty as she was, aren't you? I always liked that about her."

I felt my cheeks redden, and I hoped he didn't notice. Maybe he'd think it was the heat. After all, summer in Louisiana feels like being inside an oven.

"I've been renting this place for several months now," he said. A dog crossed the yard and trotted over. It lifted one ear toward the sound of Jack's voice and then sat by his feet. "Hey, jolie," he said, bending down to pat her on the head. She was stocky, and speckled brown and gray like granite, with expressive ears and a docked tail. Her eyes narrowed in my direction, and she let out a half-hearted bark.

"A Catahoula," I said, holding my hand out for her to sniff.

"Yeah," Jack said, and she snorted.

"The lawyer never mentioned anyone renting this house," I said.

"Probably didn't know. Vergie had only been living in the city for about six months. She let me stay here for practically nothing, just so it wouldn't sit empty."

"In the city?"

"She was staying in New Orleans with a friend," he said, still stroking the dog's fur. "Didn't you know?"

"We were out of touch for a long time."

"I was awful sad to hear about her," he said. "They broke the mold when they made Vergie."

It bothered me that he knew more about my own grandmother than I did. And it hurt when I thought about how I'd avoided this place for so long, how I'd gone so many years without seeing the woman who had been like a second mother to me. I pushed the regrets away to stop my voice from cracking. "I spent every summer here when I was a kid," I said, sitting down next to him on the porch steps.

Ordinarily, I wouldn't let my guard down with a stranger, but the drive and the humidity had left me weak. With no breeze, the air was stifling, and I was grateful for any patch of shade.

"Me, too," he said. "I mean, I used to work for her. Started when I was about seventeen."

"Really?"

"Yard work and odd jobs. She was trying to keep me out of trouble, I think."

I smiled, wondering if that was true.

"Strange," he said. "We could have met years ago. Wouldn't that be something?" He stared at me for a while, like he might recognize me.

Maybe that was it. I glanced away.

The dog pressed her nose against my thigh. She squinted at me and then dropped her head on my knee as I scratched her ears.

"You all right?" he asked. "You look a little pale." He set those eyes on me again, and I felt like I'd burn up right there on the porch. He seemed to genuinely care, despite the fact that I'd accused him of trespassing.

"It's the heat," I said. "I'm not used to it any more."

He smiled, revealing dimples that were made for disarming people like me. "Where are you coming from?"

"Raleigh." My eyes drifted to the inside of his forearm, to his tattoo. I had a soft spot for tattoos—especially the kind only partially revealed by clothing. I didn't want him to catch me staring, though, so I looked back to the dog, who had started to drool on my knee. Apparently she'd decided I was no longer a threat.

"How about a glass of water?" he asked, touching my arm.

"Sure, thanks."

He stared at me like he thought I might faint. "It's a hot one today. I'd bring you inside, but the A/C units have been acting up, blowing fuses every chance they get. I'm trying to give them a rest."

I leaned against the stair railing, feeling light-headed.

"At least out here there's a breeze," he said. He disappeared into the house, leaving me on the porch. I pictured myself sitting in a rocker with Vergie, sipping tea and eating macaroons. It didn't seem possible that someone else could live here now.

"Here you go, cher," Jack said, sitting next to me again.

Cher. I fought back a smile, thinking that was likely his way of getting anything he wanted from a woman. There probably weren't many that could turn down the likes of him.

Jack's knee brushed mine, and I instinctively moved my leg away. "You know you have to leave," I said. I tried to be as nice as possible while standing my ground. Being a landlord was not anywhere on my to-do list.

"Usually it takes longer for women to tell me that."

"Sorry," I told him. "I'm no good at evicting people."

"Then don't," he said, his voice light. He smiled again.

"I'm not in the business of renting. I'm here to fix this house and sell it. I'm afraid that means you have to leave."

"But I live here," he said. "You know how hard it is to find nice places out this way?"

"Didn't you think that when the landlady died, you should start looking for a new house?" I leaned against the banister, fanning myself. "I'm sorry that this comes as a surprise to you, but I've got no other option."

He shrugged. "I'd paid Miss Vergie up through the next few months. I figured I had a couple more weeks to worry about moving."

I tried to wrap my head around the logic of that. It was hard to give him a firm glare when he gazed at me with those woeful eyes.

Like a calf in a hailstorm, Vergie would have said. "How about if I refund your rent?"

He ran his hands through his hair. "How about you keep renting to me," he suggested.

I laughed but then saw he was serious. "I'm no landlord, Mr. Mayronne. I don't have time for that kind of responsibility."

"How hard can it be, cher? You just collect a check now and then."

"I don't live around here. I can't keep this place up."

"I've been keeping it up just fine." He sounded insulted. "You think I called Miss Vergie every time a pipe burst? I've been fixing things up all the while. You wouldn't need to be nearby."

The place did look OK, but he'd done some half-assed repairs. A couple of boards on the porch were unfinished, recently replaced. The paint on the door and window sills was fresher than the rest, making the older paint look dirty. The inside was probably peppered with spots that needed a matching coat of paint or a few finishing nails. People were constantly doing do-it-yourself repairs only halfway, which always meant more work for me.

"You'll have to find another place," I said.

The dog sat up, ears flat.

"But Enza, you can't just kick me out." His eyes were bright blue, but they flashed darker as he became flushed. When the light hit them, I saw little flecks of green, and I wanted to lean in for a better look. I was helpless around good-looking, charming guys like him, and I knew if he caught on to that, he'd try anything to stay.

Read more about Enza and Jack in
Bayou My Love: A Bayou Sabine Novel:
bit.ly/bayoumylove

Acknowledgments

A special thank you always goes to my family and friends: you are my cheerleaders, and you fill my life with the very best stories. A big thanks goes to Andrew, who listens to my crazy ideas and tells me to keep going. Thanks always to Katie Rose Guest Pryal, for being my best and most trusted beta reader (and for always nudging me forward, even when it requires Dickel). I'm especially grateful to Maggie Dallen for first publishing *Just the Trouble I Needed* in the collection *Dog Eared Love*. As always, thank you to my readers—you keep my writerly world spinning.

About the Author

Lauren divides her time between writing, teaching, and printmaking. She is the author of the Bayou Sabine Series, which includes the novels *Bayou My Love* and *Bayou Whispers.*

Originally from South Carolina, she has worked as an archaeologist, an English teacher, and a ranger for the National Park Service. She earned her MFA in creative writing from Georgia College & State University, and her MFA in Book Arts from The University of Alabama.

She won the *Family Circle* short fiction contest, was a finalist for the Novello Festival Press First Novel Award, and was nominated for an AWP Intro Award. She's a sucker for a good love story and is happiest when she writes comedy and romance. She lives in North Carolina, where she's at work on the next novel in the Bayou Sabine series.

sign up for Lauren's author newsletter,
Writing Down South:
tinyletter.com/firebrandpress

Books by Lauren Faulkenberry

- BAYOU MY LOVE
- BACK TO BAYOU SABINE
- BAYOU WHISPERS
- JUST THE TROUBLE I NEEDED
- BENEATH OUR SKIN and Other Stories

www.laurenfaulkenberry.com

Made in the USA
Columbia, SC
19 March 2022

57889643R00071